A MAN LIKE NO OTHER

Raven Woman looked Golden Hawk up and down, then smiled and said, "I see that you want me. So I wait. But you do not approach me. Is it true what they say—that Golden Hawk only *looks* at women?"

"I'm a man like any other," he said.

"No. You are not like any other. You are not a true Comanche," Raven Woman said, and, with one quick glance at him, disappeared inside his hut.

He followed her.

She had lit a candle and was lying on his blanket, naked. As the flickering light played over her, he caught his breath. From head to toe, she was a deep lustrous brown. Her long, dark hair spilled over her gleaming shoulders and coiled around her large, firm breasts.

She was waiting for him to prove what kind of a man he was. And Golden Hawk had a long, long night in which to do it. . . .

Ⓢ **SIGNET** (0451)

HOLD ON TO YOUR SADDLE!

☐ **THE SHOOTIST, by Glendon Swarthout.** (144953—$2.95)
☐ **SKINNER, by F.M. Parker.** (138139—$2.75)
☐ **LUKE SUTTON: OUTRIDER, by Leo P. Kelley.** (134869—$2.50)
☐ **THE SEARCHER by F. M. Parker.** (141261—$2.75)
☐ **NO GOD IN SAGUARO by Lewis B. Patten.** (141687—$2.75)
☐ **THE ARROGANT GUNS, by Lewis B. Patten.** (138643—$2.75)
☐ **GUNS AT GRAY BUTTE, by Lewis B. Patten.** (135741—$2.50)
☐ **THE RAWHIDERS by Ray Hogan.** (143922—$2.75)
☐ **CORNUDA'S GUNS, by Ray Hogan.** (133382—$2.50)
☐ **THE DOOMSDAY CANYON, by Ray Hogan.** (139216—$2.75)

Prices slightly higher in Canada

Buy them at your local bookstore or use this convenient coupon for ordering.

NEW AMERICAN LIBRARY
P.O. Box 999, Bergenfield, New Jersey 07621

Please send me the books I have checked above. I am enclosing $_____
(please add $1.00 to this order to cover postage and handling). Send check
or money order—no cash or C.O.D.'s. Prices and numbers are subject to change
without notice.

Name_____

Address_____

City_____State_____Zip Code_____
Allow 4-6 weeks for delivery.
This offer is subject to withdrawal without notice.

GOLDEN HAWK

Will C. Knott

A SIGNET BOOK

NEW AMERICAN LIBRARY

PUBLISHER'S NOTE

This novel is a work of fiction. Names, characters, places, and incidents either are the product of the author's imagination or are used fictitiously, and any resemblance to actual persons, living or dead, events, or locales is entirely coincidental.

SIGNET, SIGNET CLASSIC, MENTOR, ONYX, PLUME, MERIDIAN AND NAL BOOKS are published by New American Library, 1633 Broadway, New York, New York 10019

First Printing, September, 1986

1 2 3 4 5 6 7 8 9

PRINTED IN THE UNITED STATES OF AMERICA

Golden
Hawk

Prologue

It was the time of the Comanche Moon.

Astride their ponies, the four Comanches cantered along the ridge for a hundred yards or so, then halted. Impassively the warriors watched the single covered wagon inch across the grassland below. The long iron tips of their fourteen-foot lances gleamed in the slanting rays of the setting sun, the bright feathers woven into their ponies' manes and tails tugging in the light wind.

The chief of the war party wore a headdress fashioned from the head of a buffalo, the horns sweeping up in a barbaric arc. His legs, clear to the tops of his thighs, were encased in buckskin leggings. From their seams hung brass beads and fringes. On his left arm was his sacred shield, and his bow was strung across his broad chest. He was naked except for his dark breechclout and the leggings, and his proud savage face was framed by straight black hair, his forehead and cheeks slashed with war paint.

The wagon's destination was soon clear. It was heading for a narrow patch of oak lining a river-bank at least two miles distant. With a barely discernible nudge of his inner thigh, the war chief turned his pony and rode back off the rise, his three companions following.

There was no need for discussion. Each savage knew well enough how to proceed. After hob-bling their ponies in the thick brush along the river bottom, they would work their way back up to the white eyes' camp. Though it would be dark then, the moon's luminous disk would have lifted into the night sky, casting a silvery sheen over the landscape, turning black night into phan-tom day.

And by its light the Comanches would have no difficulty launching their attack.

Drawn by two mules and trailing a single milch cow, the wagon halted under a towering oak be-side the Navasota River. Astride powerful Ken-tucky-bred horses, Amos Thompson and his son, Jedidiah, pulled up and dismounted. The boy was fourteen—four years older than his sister, Annabelle, who clambered quickly down from the wagon with her mother. Their mother's name was Charity. She was a woman of thirty-five, still pretty, with blond hair, dark-blue eyes, and a ready, mischievous smile.

The family had journeyed across Ohio, then through St. Louis, heading for this new republic of Texas. Amos Thompson had fought with the Texans against the Mexicans. On his return, he had told all who would listen of the lush, expansive land of rolling prairies and river-watered woodlands he had found. Now, at last, he had returned with his family to this lush, bountiful land.

Working as rapidly as they could in the growing dusk, the Thompsons set about making camp. A distant wolf howled. The lonely sound caused the boy Jed to glance nervously over at his father, who was leading the mules to a pasture behind the wagon. His father appeared to take no notice of the howling wolf, so the boy continued on through the timber, leading the two saddle horses to a lush pasture close along the riverbank. Once Jed let them loose to graze, he glanced up at the brilliant moon. It had made finding his way a simple matter. The flood of moonlight pouring down through the leafy canopy was almost bright enough to read by.

After supper Amos Thompson reminded Jed to hobble the horses, then set off to check on the mules. Jed hurried down through the ghostly timber, hobbled the two horses, then moved back up through the trees, heading toward the sound of his sister's singing. In the clear, windless night, her song carried beautifully. She had a voice as clear and bright as birdsong in the spring. Annabelle was very proud of her voice; so though the rest of the family loved to hear her sing, they were careful not to praise her too highly. It would not do for Annabelle to become too proud.

Pulling up suddenly, Jed thought he glimpsed movement below him in the trees—shadowy forms caught in the moonlight. It was deer, or possibly game of some kind. From off to his left came what sounded like the short, yipping bark of a wolf. He was certain he saw a pair of eyes gleaming in the darkness. Wolves! His heart skipped a beat, and a premonitory dread fell over him.

He looked more closely, but saw no shadows, no gleaming eyes this time. Instead there came from above him in the trees the echoing call of a meadowlark. Jed shrugged off his uneasiness and headed for the comforting glow of the campfire.

Near the wagon, his father and mother were conversing softly. Unwilling to disturb them, Jed sat cross-legged in front of the fire's crackling warmth. His parents were discussing a homesite. Jed could tell that from the way his father waved his arm as he talked. He saw his mother lean close to her husband and say something, her voice a soft, comforting drawl. Jed's father replied, and she laughed softly and poked him in a playful way long familiar to Jed.

It was a moment Jed would remember for the rest of his life.

Abruptly Jed's father reached into the wagon and took out the family Bible. Jed was not surprised. He'd been expecting his father to read to them from it from the moment they first halted in this beautiful oak grove.

Jed glanced over as the cow blatted. Tethered to the wagon's tailgate, she was no longer chewing her cud. She was holding up her head alertly, her tail drooping straight down. It was those wolves he had seen out there, Jed figured. The cow could smell them.

Annabelle stepped down from the wagon to join her mother and father. She had been combing out her hair while she sang, and now it hung down her back, gleaming in the bright moon like a single fold of golden silk.

Jed's father glanced over at Jed and beckoned him closer. "Get over here, Jed."

Jed got up and joined his family.

"Guess what, Jed?" his mother said, smiling warmly down at him. She reached over and tousled his sandy hair. It was a caress, really, and warmed Jed. "We're thinking of settling right here."

"I think that'd be fine," Jed said.

"We'll build on that knoll over there," his father added, pointing eagerly at a slight rise beyond the oak grove. His voice was resonant with happiness. "It should give us a real fine view of the river."

"I suppose so," said Annabelle, "but it will sure be lonely until we get neighbors."

"That won't take long," assured her mother.

"And now, children," Amos Thompson told them, "it seems to me that this would be a good time to hear the word of God—and to give thanks to the Almighty for showing us safely to this golden land."

Their father led them over to the fire. Jed sat down cross-legged in the grass next to Annabelle, and the three of them waited for Amos Thompson to find an appropriate passage. Flipping the pages swiftly, he held the Bible up so that its pages could catch both the light from the fire and the marvelous brightness of the moon. It had risen so high by this time that it was well above the tallest of the oak trees.

"What're you goin' to read, Pa?" Jed asked, pushing a shock of hair out of his eyes.

"I'm looking," his father said, his finger running down one page.

"Proverbs," said Annabelle. "Try Proverbs, Pa."

Frowning in concentration, Amos Thompson leaned closer to the fire to read over silently what he had selected. As he did so, a wolf howled from the timber just behind the wagon. He glanced up in some annoyance, then looked over at Jed. "That wolf sounds pretty close, Jed."

Jed nodded. "I think I saw a few when I came up from the river."

"Guess we'd better bring the horses and mules in closer—and keep the fire blazing."

Jed nodded.

As his father turned his attention back to the Bible, an arrow thumped hollowly into his back, slamming him forward into the fire. The sparks leapt up in a sudden shower as the night came alive with the soul-chilling cries of an Indian war party.

Jed jumped up as a warrior, not ten feet away, flung himself at him, knocking him backward. On his back, Jed struggled with a sweaty, stinking aborigine made even more fearsome by a buffalo-horn headdress. The Indian had a tomahawk in his right hand and was slashing down with it, trying to bash out Jed's brains. Twice the blade slammed off the side of Jed's head. Jed winced and snapped his head back and forth, desperately trying to break free. But the Indian was powerful and stocky, his weight effectively pinning Jed to the ground.

Jed spit in the Indian's face. Furious, the Indian dropped his tomahawk and reached back for the knife in his belt. That was all the advantage Jed needed. As the Indian shifted his weight, Jed heaved him off and rolled away. Snatching up the discarded tomahawk, Jed swung it wildly and caught the Indian on the side of his head. Then Jed heaved himself upright.

High, terrified screams riveted him—his mother's voice!

Turning, he saw her down on the ground, two Indians holding her while another dropped his breechclout. Jed raced to his mother's aid, flinging himself at the closest Indian. Catching him in the small of his back, Jed bore him to the ground, slashing clumsily at him with the tomahawk. He caught the Indian in the shoulder, felt the impact as the blade sank deep. Blood spurted from the wound. Leaping up, he flung himself at the other Indian holding his mother. But suddenly a war club crashed down on his head. Lights exploded deep within his skull. His knees sagged. He dropped to the ground, barely conscious. When he tried to get up, he couldn't move. The earth spun sickeningly under him and he drifted off into darkness. . . .

*   *   *

He didn't know how long he lay there, but gradually he became aware of someone kicking him repeatedly in the back and side. The punishment was insistent, continuing until he was fully awake. He opened his eyes and saw that his tormentor was the Indian with the bison headdress. Reaching down, the Indian grabbed his hair and yanked him to a sitting position, then bound his wrists and ankles with rawhide. The narrow strips bit cruelly into his flesh. Then the Indian flung him facedown onto the ground and rejoined his fellow warriors.

Turning his head, Jed saw his mother over near the wagon. The savages had stripped her and bound her spread-eagled to stakes pounded into the soft ground. As one Indian got down upon her, the remaining three squatted close, patiently waiting their turn. This was why the Indian with the horned headdress had worked so hard to arouse Jed.

He wanted Jed to watch.

Tears of rage welled into his eyes, and he turned his head and closed his eyes to block it out. But he couldn't stop his ears. For what seemed like an eternity, he lay there listening, first to his mother's shrill screams, then to her last awful, choking sobs. She sounded like a little girl whose heart had been broken.

Some time later another Indian walked over and began kicking Jed methodically about the head and shoulders. Jed turned himself over and flung up his bound hands to ward off the blows.

Impatiently the Indian grabbed his hair and yanked him up on his feet as the other three Indians started to walk over.

Looking beyond them, Jed saw Annabelle bound hand and foot beside the lifeless, naked body of their mother. There was a bloody smear in his sister's golden hair where one of the Indians had clubbed her unconscious. Jed's father was still sprawled across the fire, most of his clothes burned off, his chest and groin black and peeling from the flames that had roasted him. An arrow protruded from his back and his skull had been staved in from the blow of a Comanche toma-hawk. His hair was matted darkly where the blood had exploded from his skull.

Both his parents had been scalped.

Choking back a sob of rage, Jed glared back at the four Indians. They had halted within a few feet and were studying him speculatively. The Indian wearing the bison-horn headdress was ap-parently their leader. All were dressed in breech-clouts and long deerskin moccasins that came up to their bare thighs. Across their hairless faces and foreheads, they had daubed broad black stripes. One brave had black rings around his eyes; another had accented the hollows in his cheeks, giving him a frightening, skull-like look. The brave next to that one had woven a single yellow feather into his scalp lock. A long scar ran from his left shoulder clear to his waist.

Jed knew they were going to kill him. He waited grimly, hoping only that they do it quickly.

The war chief took a step closer to Jed, a long,

gleaming knife in his hand. Abruptly he bent and sliced through the rawhide binding Jed's ankles and wrists. Then he spoke to Jed in Comanche, indicating with a motion of his right hand that Jed should attack him. The Comanche's voice was taunting.

With a sudden, despairing cry of rage, Jed rushed at him, head down, slamming as hard as he could into his waist. Jed heard the air explode from the startled Indian's mouth. Flailing wildly at him, Jed bore the Indian back. He felt his knuckles cracking against the Indian's bared ribs. He kept punching, waiting for the Indian to slip a knife into his side or for the sharp blade of tomahawk to come slicing down through his skull.

Instead, the Indian broke back and spun free of him, laughing. Confused, Jed saw the other Indians poking one another in admiration. Jed lunged at the Indian with the long scar. This one broke back also, laughing. The rest circled him alertly, watching, noting with obvious approval Jed's fierce demeanor.

Abruptly the war chief rushed close and tapped Jed on the shoulder.

"Ah-he!" the Comanche cried, ducking nimbly away. "I claim him!"

Jed understood none of this and again lashed out at the Indian. But, tired of the sport, the four closed swiftly about him. In less than a few seconds, Jed's bloody wrists and ankles were once more bound tightly with rawhide, and he was flung to the ground.

Jed watched helplessly as the Indians looted

the wagon. Their family trunks were hurled from the wagon and axed open, their contents scattered over the ground. Cooking utensils came clattering out, along with tools and other goods, many to be snatched up eagerly by the Indians. A mirror was grabbed by the brave with the black war paint around his eyes, and he began dancing around, holding the mirror to his face.

A moment later the Indian in the horned headdress clambered down from the wagon carrying his father's most prized possession: the Hawken rifle he had purchased in St. Louis. Uttering a triumphant cry, the war chief held up the rifle for all to see. As the others crowded around jealously, the Indian ran his fingers along the thirty-six-inch barrel, then caressed the rifle's slender, beautifully turned hardwood stock, his obsidian eyes gleaming.

A final explosion of destructive fury followed. Crowding about the milch cow, the warriors killed her with their battle axes in a swift, bloody assault. Next, they plucked burning brands from the fire and set the wagon ablaze. Savagely resplendent in gingham and calico strips and the colorful profusion of ribbons they had found in the trunks, the Indians brought up their ponies.

Without ceremony, the war chief grabbed Jed and flung him onto the pony's back, across a saddle blanket that stank of sweat and piss. A sharp dagger of pain exploded in his chest. It felt as if he had crushed one of his ribs. He was yanked brutally upright, and his ankles were lashed together with a horsehair lariat passed under the pony's belly. A rawhide leash was snapped tightly about his neck. He couldn't breathe, and his vision blurred as he gasped for air. The Indian loosened the noose roughly, just enough to let air pass through his throat. The tether was fiendishly effective, Jed realized. If he fell off the horse or tried to run away, he'd be throttled instantly.

The Comanche chief mounted up in front of Jed and proudly brandished the Hawken rifle, the leash grasped firmly in his hand. Jed saw Annabelle, conscious now, flung roughly onto another pony and tied to it just as securely. The war party's chief kicked his pony to a canter and in a moment the blazing wagon and river were behind them as they rode through the moonlit night, the Indians driving the two fine Kentucky-bred horses ahead of them.

As they pounded on over the prairie, Jed glanced up at the full moon. It was climbing still higher into the sky, sending a bright, shimmering light over the vast, undulating grasslands that extended clear to the horizon. Across this fabulous landscape they swept, the sea of grass leaving not a trace as it closed in behind them.

Jed's heart sank. He and his sister were the helpless captives of murderous Indians. From the time he was able to sit at his elders' knees and listen to stories of such captures, Jed had dreaded such a fate. Only this wasn't a story told by an old man smoking a clay pipe.

This was real, and it was happening to him and Annabelle.

—1—

Alonzo Gonzales, the one they called Saddle Maker, had only one eye. His missing right eye had been gouged out by a blazing stick wielded by a Comanche woman moments after he was dragged into the village. In addition, his right arm was withered and crooked. He'd been dragged for two miles behind a racing war pony ridden by a young Comanche anxious to show his contempt for all Mexicans. The arm had been nearly torn from its socket and had snapped in three places. Almost as an afterthought, the Comanches crowding around had castrated him. Not one of the fractures in his arm had healed properly.

Yet Alonzo was tolerated now, even honored, for despite his crippled arm and the loss of one eye, his fine workmanship and skill in fashioning saddles for his Comanche masters was unrivaled by any other saddlemaker in the Kwahadi band.

It was ten years after Jed and Annabelle had

been abducted that the crippled and half-blind Alonzo left the Comanche village to bring Jed the news of his sister's plight. He found Jed on an oak-studded knoll just above the horse herds, practicing with his throwing knife, sending the blade with remarkable accuracy at a tree twenty feet away. Six-feet-two now—a blond giant of a Comanche—Jed slipped his knife into his sheath at the back of his neck and turned to greet Alonzo.

Alonzo spoke rapidly in Spanish, for Jed was now as fluent in that tongue as he was in Comanche. Jed listened with growing fury. Annabelle had been shamefully rejected by the famed war chief Wolf Stalker, and had been left with contemptuous cruelty in front of Buffalo Hump's lodge. The news of her return was spreading now through the village with the speed and virulence of a smallpox epidemic.

When Alonzo had finished, Jed's lean, bronzed face was dark with suppressed fury.

"Are you sure Wolf Tracker *threw* her from his pony?" he asked, his quiet voice vibrant. "Perhaps that part of it was just gossip."

Alonzo shook his head sadly. "It was not gossip, *amigo*. Many saw the Comanche pig do this. Wolf Tracker made sure of that. He was very angry."

Jed swore then, bitterly, and turned to look in the direction of the village, a cluster of tepees along the river a mile or so below him. In his mind's eye he visualized the scene as Alonzo had related it to him: Wolf Tracker wheeling his pony and riding haughtily away, proclaiming loudly to all within earshot that he had had enough of Sky Woman. Her tongue was sharp, her body cold. With an eloquence that every Comanche would recall from this day forward, he had insisted that the icy wind from the north was warmer than her arms, that she was no comfort to a warrior and would bring him only crazed or bent children.

"Buffalo Hump is in disgrace," Alonzo went on. "It is said he has beat Sky Woman repeatedly since her return. She will not wail, however. And it is said she refuses to ask forgiveness of Buffalo Hump for the shame she has brought him."

Jed didn't doubt that. He knew his sister well enough to know how proud and unwilling she was to bend to the will of her Comanche father— or any Comanche, for that matter. Jed rested his hand on Alonzo's shoulder. "Thank you for coming this far to tell me."

"I thought you should know, *amigo*," Alonzo replied simply.

Alonzo knew well Jed's hatred of the Comanches. It was a loathing the two men shared. In the fire of this ferocious, mutual hatred, they had forged a trust that bound them as closely as brothers.

"What will you do?" Alonzo asked. "Things will go bad for Sky Woman now."

"I will go see her tonight," Jed replied. "She will need comfort."

It was late, well past midnight. Yet Jed knew his sister would be waiting anxiously for him to come to her—as he had so often before during these long, terrible years of their captivity. Jed threw a few pebbles softly against the side of Buffalo Hump's tepee.

Annabelle slipped out of the tepee. The two embraced, greeting each other softly in English, a tongue they refused to let die. To hear its familiar cadences was the only real assurance they had. It told them that no matter how they stank or how many parasites crawled on their bodies, they were still members of a civilization to which they would someday return.

Jed stepped back and peered closely at Annabelle's face. She was twenty years old now, and over the years she had grown more beautiful, the news of which had spread far beyond the Staked Plains. But tonight her beauty was marred. Her jaw was swollen and her eyes were red from too much crying. There was a dark, purplish bruise on one cheekbone. Seeing all this, Jed drew her close again and held her for a long moment. She clung to him gratefully in return.

Jed gently released her. "Alonzo has told me everything. I know this Wolf Tracker," he told her. "He was one of those who took us."

"Yes," she hissed. "I remember."

"I didn't think you'd be able to stomach him. No matter how many ponies he gave Buffalo Hump. Is it true? Did he let Buffalo Hump keep the ponies?"

"Yes. But Buffalo Hump says that only increases his shame."

"Alonzo told me. And that's why Wolf Tracker didn't take them back. Was he cruel?"

"He stank worse than Buffalo Hump," she hissed. "Like all Comanches, he is a woman beater." She bared her shoulder so Jed could see the welts.

"I'll kill him."

"Yes. Someday I hope you will."

Again they embraced. There were few words that might give either of them comfort. All they had was each other. If a Comanche had come upon them at that moment, he might have thought them two gods from another world—so unlike the squatter, darker Comanches were they.

Though Annabelle had stopped growing years before, she was still taller than most Comanche women. In the soft moonlight, her light-blue eyes still sparkled and her long hair shone like burnished gold. Jed himself had filled out magnificently, his shoulders broad, his long limbs tapering. Like his sister's, his eyes were blue, but a darker shade, one that resembled closely those of his mother. His thick shock of hair shone as brightly as Annabelle's, and both of their faces had the same sharp, angular lines of their parents, striking evidence of their common parentage.

"I heard Buffalo Hump has not been kind," Jed told her.

"He no longer beats me, but he won't speak to me directly. Hank-of-Hair now tells me what he wants, and she finds this very amusing. I'm afraid, Jed! This can't last long. I think Buffalo Hump is going to do something about me. He has to. I'm too much of an embarrassment now. Oh, Jed, if only we could escape!"

Annabelle was right. So far, she had managed to avoid marriage to the succession of braves who had courted her. Known as Tah-noh-wa, Sky Woman, she was the favorite of the respected Buffalo Hump, her Comanche father. As a result, she had been able to prevail upon him to refuse the bounty offered in return for her hand. These refusals, however, had cost Buffalo Hump many fine presents, once even a small herd of ten spotted ponies, each one so swift and powerful that the old man had wept bitter tears at the thought of losing such a prize.

So it was that when Wolf Tracker left his most prized buffalo pony in front of Buffalo Hump's lodge, the old chief had been unable to resist and had given Sky Woman to the young chief. That had been a week before, and now Sky Woman had returned in shame. She had become an embarrassment, a daughter no longer welcome in Buffalo Hump's lodge.

Annabelle and Jed could wait no longer.

"I promise," Jed told his sister. "As soon as the nights are dark again, I'll kill Two Horns, and we'll escape."

"Do we have to wait till then?"

"We've waited this long. Another month won't matter. Do what you can to please the old man. You've been able to do so in the past."

Annabelle nodded wearily. "All right, Jed. But no longer than a month. It doesn't matter if I make it safely as long as I'm free of these savages for just a few days. Their brutality is creeping into my soul, despite all I do to keep it out. I was as savage as Wolf Tracker when I fought him. He took me repeatedly, but I gave him no comfort and tore cruelly at him with my tongue. I'm surprised he didn't kill me. Oh, Jed, I don't like what I'm becoming."

Jed nodded bleakly. He understood fully. Awash in this Comanche culture, he felt much the same. "Be ready, then," he told her. "When the Comanche moon vanishes from the sky, we'll leave these savages behind."

She flung herself gratefully into his arms, then turned and vanished into Buffalo Hump's lodge.

Jed slipped silently back through the camp, aware that he and Annabelle had little chance of making good their escape from this remote band of Comanches. But that didn't matter as long as Jed was able to repay his debt to Two Horns, the leader of the war party that had taken them all those years ago. Annabelle was right, their escape would be worth it if only it enabled them to breathe freely for a few, precious days.

Even that would be enough.

Holding on to his patched sombrero, Alonzo cut through the tall grass. As he hurried along, the beautiful spotted ponies—as wild and graceful as antelope—reared and spilled out of his way. He found Jed bent closely over the hoof of a white-maned paint, examining it carefully. Dropping the hoof, Jed turned at Alonzo's approach. A premonition of trouble stirred within him when he saw the look on his friend's face. Slapping the pony's rump, Jed sent him cantering back to his fellows.

"What is it, Alonzo?" Jed asked. "Your face says trouble."

Panting, Alonzo pulled up in front of Jed. "It is José Santiago, the Comanche trader. He is here. He has made a trade with Buffalo Hump for your sister!"

Jed pulled Alonzo closer. "What did you say?"

"It is true. *Madre de Dios!* It is true!"

"When?"

"Last night. It is all over the camp. Everyone knows what Buffalo Hump will get in return for Sky Woman. Twenty horses, it is said. A fine rifle. A mirror! Many red beads! Sacks of coffee, sacks of sugar, and a keg of whiskey. Already Buffalo Hump is drunk. He sits in his piss and moans and laughs while Hank-of-Hair weeps."

"Is Annabelle gone already?"

"She is with Santiago's people now. Soon Santiago will leave with her."

"Where is he?"

"He has many goods and is trading for buffalo robes and pelts throughout the band." Alonzo pointed to a distant clump of cottonwood on the horizon. "Their wagons are over there, in those trees near the river."

"I will take her from this Comanchero."

"I do not think you will, *amigo.* She is guarded by many men with rifles. They know of you and what you will want to do."

"How could this be?"

"There is much talk of this in the village. All the Kwahadi know of your great love for your sister."

"It doesn't matter. I will see her. The Comancheros can't deny me that much."

Alonzo shrugged. "Good luck, *amigo*." He turned and hurried back toward the village, leaving a trail of milling, nervous horses in his wake.

Jed wasted no time. He ran down a pony, threw a grass bridle over his snout, and swung onto its bare back. Without any apparent movement of his knees or hands, he swung the pony about and urged it to a quick gallop toward the dim cluster of wagons on the horizon.

They were drawn up in a semicircle to take advantage of the cottonwoods' shade. Four mounted Comancheros were drawn up in front of the wagons. They had seen him approaching. As Alonzo had warned, each rider had a rifle resting across his pommel.

Out of the bright sun rode—straight at them—a golden-haired Comanche, his breechclout fluttering behind him, his legs encased in tan moccasins that reached to his thighs. His buttocks and chest were tanned nearly black, yet his face was unmistakably Caucasian.

As Jed grew closer, the four Comancheros closed ranks and lifted their rifles. With no visible movement, Jed caused his pony to veer abruptly, cut away from, then veer past, the four Comancheros.

Dismounting in Comanche fashion, Jed saw Annabelle jump down from the first wagon. She raced through the tall grass and flung herself into his arms. The four mounted Comancheros swiftly encircled them.

Jed glanced coldly up at them. "This is my sister," he told them in Spanish. "I will speak with her now before she leaves here."

The Comancheros looked nervously at one another. Their orders had apparently been to keep Jed and Annabelle apart. That was now plainly out of the question, and they were at a loss as to what to do next.

At that moment the sound of shod hooves pounding on the thick carpet of grass came clearly to them. Jed looked up and saw José Santiago, the Comanchero chief, riding up. Jed had made some small, insignificant trades with the Comanchero chief. What he knew of him, he didn't like. How could a white man trade with Comanches? he had asked himself bitterly over the years.

"It is Santiago," Annabelle told him, shuddering.

"Why has he traded for you? Is it to set you free? To ransom you?"

"No," she said bitterly. "He can get many horses and wagons of buffalo robes, even costly furs, from a Cheyenne chief who has heard of me. I think I know the one. He visited Two Horns last fall before the buffalo hunt."

"His name?"

"I don't know his name. And this Comanchero dog will not tell me."

By that time José Santiago had reached them. Dismounting swiftly, he strode over to Jed and his sister. As he looked them up and down, he nodded shrewdly. "I tell you something," he said in reasonably good English, "I think maybe you two are not real Comanches."

"Take me with you," said Jed. "You can use me. These Comanches will sell me cheap—and I will make a fine scout."

"What do you know of this land? All you know is the Staked Plains—this small corner of it. Besides, when it comes to dealing with the Cheyenne, you will be a nuisance."

"You'll be sorry."

Santiago laughed. "Yes. That is true. I will be sorry if I take you with me."

The Comanchero leader was almost as tall as Jed, with slanted, obsidian eyes, a hawk nose, and lank hair so black it was apparent he was a mestizo, as were the rest of his men. He was dressed in reasonably clean leather riding pants, a leather vest over a filthy shirt, and a low-crowned black sombrero. His tooled-leather riding boots gleamed like washed coal, and judging from the care they received, they were his most precious possession.

"You can believe me. I promise. I go where my sister goes."

"Ees that so?"

"Yes."

Santiago glanced up at the closest rider. Catching the glance, Jed whirled. The rider was bringing down his riding crop. Jed snatched it from him, grabbed the rider's belt, and flung him from his horse. The Comanchero landed on his back with such force he simply lay there, gasping for breath.

But before Jed could deal with the others, they had leapt from their mounts and grappled him to the ground. Once they had him pinned, Santiago went down on one knee beside him and placed the barrel of his pistol into Jed's mouth. Jed heard Annabelle's terrified gasp.

"Right now I could blow your brains back out through your skull, *señor*," Santiago pointed out reasonably. "Is that what you want?"

Jed slowly shook his head.

"Then listen to me. You cannot come with me. I would be a fool to allow such a thing. I would not put it past you to help your sister escape as soon as you could manage it. Already one of my men over there is on his back, gasping for breath. No, I am afraid I must leave you here."

He withdrew the pistol from Jed's mouth and stood up then. One wave of his hand and the three men holding Jed down relaxed their grip and stepped quickly back. As Jed got slowly to his feet, the Comancheros unlimbered their revolvers and covered him warily.

"At least tell me to which tribe you are taking my sister," Jed said to Santiago.

"That would be just as foolish as taking you with me."

"Someone mentioned a Cheyenne chief."

The impassive Comanchero chief said nothing, his slanted eyes regarding Jed warily.

"Let me talk to my sister," Jed told Santiago. "Alone."

Santiago shrugged and stepped back and away from them. Waving his men back also, he turned on his heels and walked to the lead wagon, his men following him. Reaching into the wagon, Santiago pulled out a jug and passed it around. As the men drank, they watched Jed and Annabelle closely. But they were far enough away for Jed and Annabelle to speak without being overheard.

"I'm sorry," Jed told Annabelle. "I'm helpless with these men."

"You must come after me, Jed."

"I will. Somehow."

"Remember your promise? You said once that if we were separated, you wouldn't rest until you had found me and returned me to my own people."

"I remember."

"Will you make that promise again?"

"I make it again, Annabelle."

Annabelle began to cry then, unashamedly. Jed drew her close and held her tightly. He felt as if the ground were opening up beneath him. He was losing everything now, all he cared for or would ever care for. Annabelle was all the family he had left. It would be just him now, one man against a savage world of horse Indians.

The next morning, standing with Alonzo on a slight rise, he watched the Comancheros' carts lumber off, heading northwest. Annabelle was in the last wagon, leaning out and waving to Jed.

Jed waved back, his throat too constricted to

call out. Until she and the wagons were out of sight, Annabelle kept waving.

As Jed started back to the horse herds, he repeated to himself the vow he had made to his sister. It was one he'd keep. No matter how far he had to travel or how long it took him, he would find Annabelle and bring her back to her own people.

—2—

Jed stood in front of Buffalo Hump's lodge and waited patiently for the old chief to invite him in. He'd been standing there since dawn. It was now close to midday.

Twice Hank-of-Hair had peered out to see if Jed still waited, her flat, wrinkled face impassive, only her eyes showing the distress she felt. Those passing the lodge that morning seemed to take no notice of Jed's tall, patient figure. But peering around the skirts of nearby lodges, the children watched, their games forgotten. And Jed knew that excited talk of his latest impertinence had long since swept through the village.

This golden-haired giant had been a dilemma for the Antelope band from the very beginning. His cold, silent aloofness had been a constant reproach to the band's members. It reminded the old warriors, those who were now done with the warpath, of something they didn't want to ad-

mit: their ceaseless warfare destroyed families
and killed innocents. To them Jed was a melan-
choly symbol of the many sons and comrades
they had lost over the years, not to mention the
herds of fine spotted war ponies their ceaseless
warfare had devoured.

To the young warriors, however, for whom warfare against the white eyes was the chief source
of wealth and renown, Jed was an irritant. He
was a constant reminder of the frustrating limits
cruelty and force of arms could accomplish when
fighting the white man. Jed just kept on coming.
Stupidly. Indomitably. At times his unshakable
sense of superiority imparted to him a medicine
almost too powerful to challenge. Yet, cold and
aloof though Jed was, he had supporters among
the band, those Comanches who grudgingly admired his stubborn fidelity to his own people's
ways.

After Annabelle's departure, a council had con-
vened to discuss Jed's place among the People.
Scowls-at-the-People, as Jed was known by the
band's members, could no longer be thought of as
simply a slave, a harmless tender of their horse
herds. His medicine was too strong for that. And
with his sister gone, it was assumed he could no
longer be trusted.

Banishment was out of the question. The People knew this was precisely what he wanted.
Since no Comanche clan had adopted him, one
suggestion had been to castrate him. It would
most assuredly destroy Jed's medicine. Many of
their castrated Mexican captives had spent their

entire adult lives as loyal, uncomplaining slaves, as willing to defend their master's lodge from attack as any full-blooded Comanche. But castration struck many of the older chiefs as going too far. For half the night the chiefs wrangled, then broke up without coming to a decision. On only one item was there unequivocal agreement: something had to be done about Jed.

It was news of this council meeting—brought to Jed by Alonzo— that prompted Jed to seek out Buffalo Hump. The old chief's deep sorrow at trading Annabelle to Santiago was apparent to everyone in the camp. It was clear he sorely regretted his decision, and Jed was counting on this.

Throughout the morning Jed remained standing in the same spot. The hammering sun beat down on him with a merciless indifference. But he made no effort to move. An hour or so after the noon hour Hank-of-Hair stuck her head out from behind the flap and beckoned Jed inside. Showing no relief at his summons or annoyance at the long delay, Jed strode casually to Buffalo Hump's lodge, lifted the flap, and entered.

Hank-of-Hair had rolled up the tepee's skirts to get some air circulating. It made no difference. The interior of the lodge was stifling. Sitting cross-legged on his couch, Buffalo Hump was smoking his favorite clay pipe. Despite the heat, he had draped his best buffalo robe over his naked shoulders. With his pipestem, he indicated to Jed a cushion on the other side of the fire pit.

Jed sank onto it and sat back casually, crossing his legs.

It would have been a breach of courtesy for Jed to come directly to the point. Ordinarily he would have paid no attention to this Comanche custom. Now, however, he honored it to the full. He spoke to the old chief of his joy at seeing him again. He praised the quality and number of his ponies, especially those Buffalo Hump had received from the Comancheros in return for Annabelle, a sly dig Jed couldn't resist. Only when he saw the sharp glint of pain that sprang into Buffalo Hump's eyes did he regret his words.

Out of the corner of his eye, he saw Hank-of-Hair scowling at him. But Jed paid her no heed and chattered on about the unseasonably hot weather and its effect on the grass, the size of the last buffalo herd the People had sighted, and the great skill Wolf Tracker had shown in cutting out and killing the many buffalo that now filled with racks of freshly jerked meat his lodges and those of his venerable parents.

Mention of Wolf Tracker—another well-considered barb—was too much for Buffalo Hump. It stirred him enough to do away with the amenities and get straight to the business at hand.

Taking his pipe from his mouth, he asked, "Why does Scowls-at-the-People approach this old one?"

Speaking in fluent Comache, Jed replied, "I desire the protection of the most respected chief among the Antelope Comanches."

Only a quick flick of an eyebrow revealed Buffalo Hump's surprise at Jed's reply, especially the respectful manner in which he had couched it. Then Buffalo Hump's eyes narrowed. It was clear that this brother of Sky Woman wanted something.

"Scowls-at-the-People does not need the protection of this old chief," he replied, leaning back and puffing on his pipe, his lidded eyes regarding Jed warily.

"That is true," Jed agreed without batting an eyelash. "Nevertheless, he would like it. His sister would approve if she were here. She felt great warmth and affection for her old father." It took a lot out of Jed to lie in this fashion, especially to refer to this mountain of suet as his sister's father. But necessity was crowding him.

"I do not want to hear of Sky Woman," Buffalo Hump said peevishly. "She is gone from Buffalo Hump's lodge. She would not be a good and obedient woman to a brave Comanche warrior with many horses and scalps. So now she warms a Cheyenne's bed. It is done."

Showing an iron resolve, Jed did not dispute the old man. He simply nodded. "As you wish. We will not talk of Sky Woman. But I am her brother. Perhaps in me you will find the obedience and respect you did not find in her."

Buffalo Hump almost choked on the smoke he was inhaling. Jed heard Hank-of-Hair's barely audible gasp. Jed was proposing nothing less than that he take his sister's place in Buffalo Hump's affection, that he might even adopt Jed.

Buffalo Hump frowned slightly to hide his own

astonishment. "Does Scowls-at-the-People, offer this old chief the obedience and comfort Sky Woman could not?"

"Yes."

"Buffalo Hump does not believe you," the chief said bluntly, almost angrily. "You are two from the same litter."

"If the wise chief Buffalo Hump does not believe the words of Scowls-at-the-People, then Buffalo Hump must test him."

Buffalo Hump sat alertly. "And how would he test him?"

"Trial by combat."

The chief took the pipestem from his mouth and leaned closer. "To the death?"

"Yes. Unless there is no warrior in the band willing to stand against me."

That there might not be a Comanche warrior eager to test Jed in combat was preposterous. With a contemptuous wave, Buffalo Hump dismissed the notion. "Is there a brave you would challenge?" Buffalo Hump asked eagerly, his eyes alight as he envisioned the combat to follow.

Jed would have liked nothing better than to meet Two Horns in combat. But suggesting him would have been fatal to his cause. Buffalo Hump knew how much Jed hated Two Horns. By singling him out, he would immediately convince Buffalo Hump that Jed's only motive in coming to him was to avenge himself on Two Horns, not to prove his loyalty to Buffalo Hump.

"I would challenge Wolf Tracker," Jed replied.

At mention of Wolf Tracker, a quick gleam of approval leapt into the old man's eyes.

It was Wolf Tracker who had spurned Sky Woman, goading Buffalo Hump into an action he now regretted profoundly. Yet there was still much for the old chief to consider in Jed's offer, as Jed well knew.

Buffalo Hump leaned back, puffing on his pipe, his lidded eyes regarding Jed closely as he pondered. One or both men could die in this combat. If Jed were killed, it would mean only that his medicine was bad and that he lied now in protesting his loyalty to Buffalo Hump. If both men died of their wounds, it would leave matters unsettled, and the band would be without the leadership of a strong and powerful chief. But if Jed survived, Buffalo Hump would have avenged Wolf Tracker and in addition gained a son to take the place of the daughter he had just lost.

"This must be settled in council," Buffalo Hump reminded Jed cautiously. "Perhaps Wolf Tracker will not consent to do battle with Scowl-at-the-People."

"Then it might be wise for Buffalo Hump to tell Wolf Tracker what I say now."

Buffalo Hump's eyebrows raised slightly. "Speak, then."

Jed smiled coldy. "Tell him that if he refuses a challenge from the brother of Sky Woman, it will not matter how many ponies he owns or how many scalps hang from his scalp pole. His name will stink in the nostrils of his Comanche brothers."

Buffalo Hump's face paled at the prospect of delivering such a rebuke to Wolf Tracker. He was barely able to suppress his displeasure at Jed's impertinence. "I will have no need to tell Wolf Tracker this," he told Jed. "He is a brave warrior. He has counted many coup. Scowls-at-the-People would do well to consider his skill in battle."

"I have already done so."

Buffalo Hump looked shrewdly at Jed. "Listen to me now. If you survive this test, it will mean only that you have told Buffalo Hump the truth when you say you wish his counsel and his support. Nothing more will come of it."

Jed squared his shoulders. "I accept that. But perhaps in time this unworthy horse herder will be allowed to join a war party. Then he may bring back to Buffalo Hump's lodge much fine booty."

Buffalo Hump regarded Jed for a long moment, his old eyes probing deep. "Perhaps," he said at length, "but first Scowls-at-the-People must survive his trial by combat with Wolf Tracker."

Buffalo Hump glanced at Hank-of-Hair. She would give Buffalo Hump either a nod or a shake of her old head to confirm or disagree with his decision. Sometimes the old chief followed his woman's advice, sometimes he didn't. But it was always good to have Hank-of-Hair's blessing in any venture undertaken with Buffalo Hump. It took all of Jed's willpower not to turn and look at her. Buffalo Hump glanced back at Jed, his wrinkled face showing that he was relieved not to be going against his woman's will.

"Return to the horse herds," he told Jed. "See that we lose no more to the wolves. The council will meet tonight. I will send for you after it has made its decision."

Jed got up and slipped quickly out of the lodge. It had been a close call, but he knew why Buffalo Hump had accepted his proposal. This was a way for him to get back at Wolf Tracker. And if Jed did manage to kill Wolf Tracker, Buffalo Hump might then have reason to consider the advantages to be gained by adopting Jed in place of Sky Woman.

Buffalo Hump was an old man now. Soon he would need a younger, stronger brave to ride with him to the buffalo hunts.

At the next council Buffalo Hump shrewdly pointed out that if Scowls-at-the-People were not truly anxious to become a Comanche at last, he would fail in his trial by combat and the band would be rid of a troublesome slave. At once Wolf Tracker announced his eagerness to meet Scowls-at-the-People in combat. After a short debate, it was decided that this would take place the very next night. It had been a dull camp; this combat would do much to liven things up.

Before the sun set the next day, the women began to build the bonfire before which the two men would fight. By the time the moon had appeared overhead, the flames were leaping high into the night. The warriors and their families crowded around, waiting in loud anticipation for the combat to begin. Among them moved Lame Deer and Coyote Piss, taking bets. The odds overwhelmingly favored Wolf Tracker. Buffalo Hump, cautious as always, would wager only his poorest buffalo pony on Scowls-at-the-People.

In breechclout and moccasins, Jed approached the fire. In his right hand he carried a stone war club he had fashioned himself. His throwing knife was resting in its sheath behind his neck, the rawhide holding it in place knotted at his throat. The Comanche men and women who moved aside to let him pass were impressed. During his years with the People, Jed had preferred to sleep out under the stars or in a brush hut away from the village. He had maintained it was better for him to remain close to the herds he was guarding. For many of the People, therefore, this was their first good look at the tall blond slave.

Jed's pale skin had been tanned almost black by the sun and his long hair had been burnished to a pale gold. Light on his feet despite his size, he moved with an easy grace. In contrast to the squatter, darker Comanches, his tall, slim figure was striking, as were the powerful, rippling muscles that ridged his upper torso like mole tunnels. Although a slave in this camp, he strode confidently past his masters, his blade of a nose and alert eyes giving him the sharp, imperious glance of an uncaged hawk.

Once he reached the fire, he folded his arms calmly and waited. He glanced casually about him, and his eyes caught one of the Comanche girls. She was Raven Woman, the daughter of a captured Mexican woman and a Comanche brave. Her dark beauty—accentuated by her lustrous, almond-shaped eyes—had always attracted him. Among the other drab, flat-faced Comanches, she stood out like a jewel. At once Jed realized that, of all those Comanches watching, Raven Woman alone wished for his victory.

A silence fell over the spectators. Wolf Tracker stepped out of his lodge and strode through the crowd toward the bonfire, a favored bearskin cloak thrown loosely over his powerful shoulders. The Comanche had added black war paint to his eye sockets and to the hollows in his cheeks. He had covered his broad chest with sharp, angular designs, also in black and white. The purpose of Wolf Tracker's design was to increase his own medicine and strike terror into the heart of his golden-haired foe. Jed was not impressed.

Wolf Tracker came to a halt ten feet from Jed and flung aside his cloak. In his right hand he carried his war club and at his side was sheathed a long skinning knife. Quiet settled on the onlookers, and the only sound was the crackling fire.

Wolf Tracker took a few steps closer to Jed, holding his war club out in front of him. Then he crouched and began to move in a circle, warily closing in on Jed. Jed watched him patiently, a deep elation building within him. For a long, long time he had been dreaming of a chance to send one of these Comanches into hell.

Uttering a piercing, soul-shattering battle cry,

Wolf Tracker threw himself at Jed. Meeting the charge head-on, the two pounded each other brutally with their clubs. They took the blows on their forearms and shoulders, filling the air with chunks of bloody flesh. Abruptly Jed retreated. Sensing victory, Wolf Tracker rushed him. Jed dropped onto his back and lifted both feet. He tucked them into Wolf Tracker's stomach, and the startled Comanche's momentum sent him flying over Jed's head.

He came down hard on his back and for a moment could only stir dazedly. Jed flung himself on Wolf Tracker's prostrate body and pressed the handle of his war club down across the stunned Comanche's windpipe. Wolf Tracker's eyes bugged out as he waited for Jed to crush the life out of him.

The watching Comanches remained silent, waiting. They were dismayed. Jed pulled back, just enough to enable Wolf Tracker to suck in a few precious mouthfuls of air.

"Enough?" he asked the warrior.

Jed expected no such mercy from Wolf Tracker. But it wasn't necessary for Jed to kill this Comanche to prove the superiority of his medicine—and the truthfulness of his assertions to Buffalo Hump.

With a furious shake of his head Wolf Tracker refused Jed's offer. He would prefer an honorable death to a craven life as the gift of a slave. A murmur of approval swept through the hushed Comanches.

His resolve hardened, Jed pressed down on the

handle of his war club. But during that brief respite, Wolf Tracker had gathered his legs under him. Driving upward in a powerful surge, he managed to lift Jed's weight off his chest. A second later, Jed found himself flying forward over Wolf Tracker's head.

The Comanches cheered wildly as Jed struck the ground. Wolf Tracker sprang to his feet. Jed was barely able to brace himself as Wolf Tracker slammed into him violently and brought around his war club in a vicious, sweeping arc. The stone blade sliced deep into Jed's left shoulder. Ignoring the wound, Jed grabbed Wolf Tracker around the waist and drove him back striking at him with his own club. He caught the Indian in his side. The blade sliced deep—too deep. As Wolf Tracker twisted away from him, the war club's bloody handle slipped from Jed's grasp.

Blood spewed out of his wound, but the Comanche still slashed furiously at Jed, aiming for his head. Jed flung up his left forearm to ward off the blow. He thought he might have broken it, but he charged forward anyway and managed to wrest the club from Wolf Tracker's grasp and fling it aside.

They were grappling hand to hand now. Suddenly, with a triumphant cry, Wolf Tracker tucked his foot around the back of Jed's ankle and sent him sprawling. Jed's head slammed into the ground, stunning him. Instantly Wolf Tracker pinned him with one knee and brought up his long skinning knife. Jed saw it slicing down toward him. With a desperate heave, he managed to roll over. The blade sank into Jed's back, grating loudly as it struck his shoulder blade.

Wolf Tracker knocked Jed's head back around with a single, vicious swipe, then straddled Jed's chest, pinning him with both knees. This time there was to be no mercy, Jed realized. The Comanche's eyes were wild with exultation as he again flung up his knife and brought it down, aiming this time for Jed's windpipe. Jed managed to yank his neck aside a few inches. The knife plunged through Jed's neck—but missed the jugular. The blade sank into the ground. Rolling swiftly over onto the knife, Jed pulled it from Wolf Tracker's grasp. He kept on rolling, then leapt to his feet.

Heavy warm blood was flowing down his chest. He turned and ran. A great, derisive roar came from the spectators at Jed's apparent cowardice. Shouting encouragement to Wolf Tracker, they urged him to get up and finish off the white eyes. Abruptly, Jed halted and turned. Wolf Tracker was back on his feet, his retrieved club in his hand.

Calmly, Jed waited.

Seeing him standing there, blood gouting from his many knife wounds, Wolf Tracker uttered another piercing war cry and flung himself across the bloody ground toward Jed. In one single, fluid motion Jed reached back for his throwing knife and hurled it at the oncoming savage. The blade twinkled in the firelight, then buried itself in Wolf Tracker's windpipe. The Comanche's knees turned to water. Gagging on his own blood, he collapsed at Jed's feet, his fists clutching convulsively at the ground. He shuddered once, then died.

Reaching down, Jed took back his knife and wiped the blade in the dead Comanche's greasy hair. Then he placed it back in its sheath. Dimly aware of the high, moaning wail of Wolf Tracker's women, he turned. His own knees turned to rope. He collapsed to the ground. The last thing he remembered were Alonzo's dark-brown eyes peering intently at his face.

Then he closed his eyes and let the darkness claim him.

—3—

Jed was unable to recall much about the week that followed.

When he regained consciousness, he found that a cocoon of pain had coiled itself about his body. Soon after that came the fever. During brief moments of lucidity, Jed wondered which was worse, the relentless pain from his wounds or the fever that threatened to consume him. His dreams were wild, disordered excursions into a netherworld of demons and hellish visions. In one of them he was turning slowly on a spit over the coals of hell.

One night he awakened to find Hank-of-Hair's flat, wrinkled face looming close as she spooned some vile concoction through his blistered lips. Emerging from a sick sleep another time, he glimpsed Buffalo Hump gazing at him from the other side of the lodge, his impassive face obscured by the smoke from the smoldering hearth.

His head seemed to detach itself from Buffalo Hump and float free of him, filling the entire lodge with his dark, ominous visage.

The fever lifted at last, and Jed was able to sit up and move cautiously about. He felt as weak as a kitten and noted he'd lost considerable weight. After a few more days, he went outside and walked about unassisted. At last, a week later, he thanked Buffalo Hump and Hank-of-Hair for taking him into their lodge and nursing him. Then he selected a shaded spot on the other side of the stream running past the village. There—a reasonable distance from its smells and clamor—he fashioned a snug brush shelter for himself and sat for days on end, his back against a willow, slowly mending.

A succession of young chiefs, impressed by the fighting qualities Jed had demonstrated in defeating Wolf Tracker, sought him out. They were eager to have him join their war parties. Jed told them he was not yet fit to ride. Besides, since he was still only a slave, he had no war pony of his own.

It was late afternoon, and a breeze was sweeping along the river, cooling Jed deliciously, when he heard the sound of splashing. Looking downstream, he saw a familiar, hated figure splashing toward him: Two Horns.

He was limping from an old leg wound that had all but severed a tendon. Over his powerful naked shoulders he had thrown a bison cape, and he was wearing his bison headdress, a sure sign that he was about to embark on another raid south. Since Two Horns returned from that raid in Texas ten years before, he had become one of the Kwahadi's most powerful war chiefs.

He strode up to Jed and halted, staring boldly down at him. A single scar ran down one side of his face, distorting his youthful features. His wide expressive mouth curved downward in a hard, arrogant line, an accurate barometer of his outlook.

The young chieftain was openly contemptuous of any in the band who were less able than he. This attitude earned him many enemies, yet there wasn't a single warrior who would dare go against him. His more than twenty scalps, his numerous coups, his riches in horseflesh garnered during his many raids into Texas and Mexico had already brought him two strong sons and three young wives, each serving him with abject humility and great respect. Yet, despite having accomplished all this, Two Horns was only six years older than Jed.

Jed didn't get up to greet Two Horns. Nor did he raise his palm in sign of friendship. Neither did Two Horns. Both men knew better. For a moment they regarded each other silently, and Jed knew that Two Horns was recalling the occasion of their first violent meeting.

Just as Jed was.

Abruptly shifting his bison cape, Two Horns spoke to him in Comanche. "Buffalo Hump has sent me," he said.

Jed didn't reply.

"The old chief says you are eager to be a real

Comanche at last," Two Horns continued. "He thinks maybe it will be a fine thing for you to ride with Kwahadi war parties so you can prove you are good Comanche and bring him back fine booty. I think this is a good idea. Soon now I ride south with Stalking Bear and Brass Kettle and many other powerful warriors. Once again the *tejanos* are ripe for plucking. I invite you to ride with us. From my own herd, I will select for you one of my finest ponies."

"Two Horns is generous, as always," Jed replied with forced courtesy. "And to ride with such renowned warriors would be a great honor. But I am too weak as yet to mount a pony. If I were to join your raiding party, I would only slow you down. Perhaps my wounds would break open again, and I would die at last. But if you will wait only a week longer, perhaps I will join you then."

"Two Horns would wait. But the full moon will not. When it fills the night with its light, we will be in Texas. We leave tonight."

"Then I will go with you another time."

Two Horns studied Jed for a long moment. Jed knew Two Horns was trying to penetrate Jed's stoic features, looking for some sign that Jed was telling the truth. Or that he was lying. Two Horns might accept Jed's excuse that he was too weak to join his raiding party. But if he thought Jed was refusing because he was unwilling to move against his own people, that would be a different matter entirely.

"It is too bad you will not join us," Two Horns

said at last, his words sounding much like a warning. "But you are right. There will be another time. Two Horns will again ask the white-eyed horse herder to join him. But he will ask only once more."

With that warning hanging in the air like a curse, Two Horns turned and limped off. Watching the Comanche go, Jed reached back behind his neck and pulled forth his throwing knife.

The rest of the afternoon he spent whetting the blade.

Less than a week after Two Horns' departure, sensational news swept the Comanche village, the gist of it brought to Jed by Alonzo. During the night a band of Pawnees had raided their eastern pony herd, driving off more than twenty head, an act calculated to bring down upon the despised Pawnees the full wrath of the Comanche band.

At once it was agreed that the Pawnees must be punished and the ponies retrieved. Yet the ablest war chiefs had left with Two Horns. Who would lead them in pursuit of the Pawnees? One young warrior, no more than sixteen years old, immediately took up the challenge. His name was Hungry Horse, and he announced that he would bring back not only the stolen ponies, but those belonging to the Pawnees as well. Standing Elk, another young brave, joined him. Soon four other young Comanche braves had joined the war party and set about filling their medicine bags with their secret things.

Jed watched one of the braves steal across the stream to retrieve his sacred war shield from its secret hiding place. In a moment the brave vanished into a patch of willows farther down. Jed stood up, waded across the stream, and entered the village in search of Hungry Horse.

Jed found the warrior outside his parents' lodge. Hungry Horse didn't invite Jed inside. The Comanche was squat in build and at least a foot shorter than Jed. It was clear he resented Jed's height and was not anxious to share with him any glory he might soon gain. With barely disguised animus, he listened as Jed requested that he be allowed to join the punitive expedition into Pawnee country.

"Before this, many warriors ask you to join them," Hungry Horse told him sulkily, "but each time you do not go. Even Two Horns you refuse. You tell him you are not yet well enough to go with him."

"I am better now."

"In a week you have healed so much?"

"Yes."

"You are a slave, not a Comanche."

"Then I shall go as a slave."

"Where is your war pony?"

"I will get one from Buffalo Hump."

Hungry Horse's eyes became crafty. With the tiniest flicker of a smile, he said, "Good. If the old chief will let you take one of his ponies, you may come with us."

It was clear Hungry Horse expected Buffalo Hump to refuse Jed's request for a pony. By refusing to join Two Horns in his expedition south to the land of the *tejanos*, Jed had convinced Buffalo Hump and many others in the band that he wasn't sincere in his insistence that he wanted to become a true Comanche.

"I will speak to the Father of My Sister," Jed told Hungry Horse.

Once again Buffalo Hump made Jed wait outside his lodge. However, this time he sent Hank-of-Hair to beckon him inside after only a few hours. Still troubled by the knife wound, Jed slowly lowered himself onto the cushion Buffalo Hump indicated. After a suitable preamble, Jed told the old chief he was ready to join a Comanche war party, and if Buffalo Hump would provide him with a pony, his exploits would make the old warrior proud enough to adopt him as a son—just as he had earlier adopted Jed's sister.

Buffalo Hump had long suspected that Jed's apparent eagerness to become one of the People had been a deception. In the weeks since Jed left his lodge, the old chief's suspicions had only grown. It seemed clear to him that all Jed had wanted was a chance to kill Wolf Tracker.

And yet, Jed's words fell on fertile soil. Buffalo Hump had no sons to provide for him in his old age, and Jed was offering him a security he had lost when he failed to marry off Annabelle to one of the band's powerful young chiefs.

Still, Buffalo Hump's suspicions didn't die easily. He took the stem of his clay pipe out of his mouth. "Before Two Horns left, I sent him to you. I said you would ride with him to Texas and bring back to Buffalo Hump much booty. But you did not go with him."

It was an accusation, not a question.

"I was not ready then. The wound in my back makes it impossible for me to breathe at times. Even now I find it difficult."

"But the scar is healed many weeks now."

"It is not healed inside."

"I will not argue with you."

"If you still do not believe me, test me again. With those stinking Pawnees who take our horses."

The good sense of this was undeniable. Buffalo Hump studied Jed impassively. "I will give you Pink Nose," he said abruptly. "He is swift as the wind and as strong as the grizzly. Also White Tail. These are my finest ponies. Your medicine will be powerful if you ride such ponies against the Pawnee."

Jed sighed gratefully. "Scowls-at-the-People thanks the generous Buffalo Hump. On such magnificent ponies, I will count many coup for the legendary chief."

"Scowls-at-the-People talks easily of coups," Buffalo Hump remarked, doing his best to hide his pleasure at Jed's words. "We shall see." He got to his feet.

Jed got up also. Together he and Buffalo Hump left the lodge to cut out the two ponies. As Jed strode beside the old chief, he couldn't help noticing that the Comanche now appeared to take some pride in appearing with Jed. It was clear he was hoping that soon he'd be boasting of Jed's exploits.

But what Jed was promising he had no intention of delivering. Still Jed couldn't help feeling a slight twinge at his deception of the old man. But the chief and the others had to be foiled in any way, Jed reminded himself. He couldn't allow himself to show any mercy. He forced himself to remember what manner of people he was dealing with. Had Wolf Tracker killed Jed, there would have been no sorrow at his death, no wailing, only a shout of triumph and a victory dance led by Wolf Tracker and all his friends. Buffalo Hump would have shrugged and felt no pangs at the loss of the sorry pony he had wagered.

These Antelope Comanches, like all the other bands, were pitiless marauders. They had murdered Jed's parents. Buffalo Hump himself had traded off his sister without the slightest concern. To him and the rest of these savages, a woman was no more than chattel to be bought and sold like horses—except that Comanches lavished far more respect and love on their ponies than on any of their women.

A week later, Hungry Horse's war party overtook the Pawnee band in the hilly, wooded country north of the Arkansas. It hadn't been difficult to track the Pawnees. Once they put the Staked Plains behind them, they made little effort to hide their sign. Now, camped by the banks of a narrow stream, the Pawnees stationed no pickets and let the stolen ponies graze unguarded in a meadow just below their camp.

By this time Jed's skill in tracking had won over most of the Comanche warriors, all of whom were younger than he. Only Standing Elk remained aloof. Now, peering down at their camp through the timber, Hungry Horse commented to Jed on the Pawnees' lack of caution. The Pawnees' leaping campfire sent a bright glow throughout their camp, and around it the celebrating Pawnees were now dancing their victory dance, their exultant cries and boastful talk drifting clearly up through the timber.

"They have the confidence that comes with numbers," Jed responded. "There are sixteen of them and only six of us, and they are deep in Pawnee country. They do not fear an attack now. They might be waiting for other Pawnees to join them."

"How do you know such a thing?" demanded Standing Elk. Of all the members of the war party, he alone refused to accept Jed as one of them. He made no effort to hide his hostility.

"It is what I think," Jed shrugged. "But I may be wrong."

The other Comanches were not so sure Jed was wrong. "If Scowls-at-the-People is right," said Hungry Horse nervously, "what should we do? The Pawnees outnumber us greatly. We cannot wait, but if we attack now, few of us will return to our lodges."

"We will not wait."

"You mean, attack now?" asked Little Fox. He

had been the first of the war party to settle in alongside Jed as they rode from the village.

"Tonight, Little Fox," Jed told him. "But not frontally. We will nibble at their flanks, like wolves on the edge of a great buffalo herd, until we cut their numbers down to ours."

"And how do we do this?" asked Hungry Horse.

Jed settled back against a tree and calmly explained to them the plan he had been formulating since he first caught sight of the Pawnee encampment.

Judging by the North Star, it took Jed close to an hour to reach the Pawnee he had selected. The Indian was asleep, wrapped in a blanket that smelled strongly of rancid sweat. Clapping his left hand over the Pawnee's mouth, Jed struck down with his knife, slicing cleanly through the blanket. The Pawnee shuddered. Jed lifted the knife again and brought it down a second time. The Pawnee went limp. Carefully, Jed lifted his hand from the Indian's mouth. The Pawnee's head lolled to one side, his eyes staring sightlessly at Jed.

Jed listened for a second to make sure he hadn't aroused any of the other Pawnees. Then, like a large silent snake, he pulled himself on through the tall grass to the second Pawnee he had selected. Dispatching this one with the same efficiency, Jed inched his way back the way he had come. Once in the timber, he was joined by the other Comanches—all but Little Fox. They waited nervously. At last Little Fox showed up. As he had approached one of the sleeping Pawnees, he told them, the Pawnee had flung off his robe and gone to the river to relieve himself. Little Fox had followed after him, surprising him when he was most preoccupied.

The Comanches could barely contain their elation. Hungry Horse and Jed had each selected two Pawnees, the rest one each. Their deadly coups complete, Hungry Horse's war party had reduced the number of their enemies to seven. Jed's own elation was muted. The Pawnees would have done the same to him and his companions were the roles reversed, he knew. But the killing had been cold-blooded.

With Hungry Horse leading the way, they crept to the edge of the timber and waited for dawn. The Pawnees might flee without the Comanches' ponies when they found their number so drastically reduced. But even if they did, it would give Hungry Horse's war party enough scalps to mark this as a tremendous victory, one that would set their village to rejoicing.

But Jed didn't expect the Pawnees to flee.

He was right. Seconds before the first light of dawn streaked the eastern sky, cries erupted from the Pawnee camp. Grim smiles wreathed the faces of the Comanches as they gripped their weapons and watched the Pawnees running from one dead warrior to another. One of the Pawnees went down on one knee, studying the broken blades of grass, the unmistakable signs the crawling Comanches had left as they snaked their way back into the timber. The other Pawnees joined him. At once a grim war parley was held. When it broke up, one Pawnee took a step toward the timbered slope. Shaking his fist, he uttered a cry that could only be interpreted as a challenge.

Jed took it. Uttering the shrill Comanche war cry in response, he ran down the slope through the timber and broke out onto the grass, heading toward the gesticulating Pawnee. Behind him, the rest of the war party followed, rending the air with their war cries. Arrows sang past Jed. One snapped through his flying hair. Twenty yards before Jed reached the foremost Pawnee, he threw his knife. The blade sunk into the brave's heart. He staggered, then collapsed back into the deep grass. Flashing past him, Jed withdrew his knife and, with his shoulder still down, met the charge of another Pawnee and threw him over his shoulder.

Spinning, Jed buried his knife into the Pawnee's belly, then sliced upward. He almost lost the knife when the blade struck the Pawnee's breast-bone. Pulling the blade free, Jed ducked away from the surge of blood that followed out after it. Jed glanced up. He was in the midst of a hand-to-hand melee.

A few feet away, Little Fox was struggling with a Pawnee twice his size. Jed flung himself at the Pawnee, caught him about the waist, and flung him to the ground, then rolled free. Leaping astride the downed Pawnee's shoulders, Little Fox finished him off with a terrible blow that shattered his skull like an overripe melon.

Jed got to his feet as Little Fox cried out a

warning. Jed turned in time to see a Pawnee racing at him, his lance lowered. Parrying the lance with one hand, Jed danced lightly to one side and slashed out with his knife. The astonished Pawnee swept past Jed, his head nearly severed from his shoulders. Staggering a few paces, the Pawnee dropped his lance and crumpled facedown into the grass.

In that instant the battle was over.

Jed looked swiftly about him. All six of his blood-spattered companions were staring around at one another, their painted faces revealing their elation. Jed had no difficulty at all reading in their expression what they were thinking.

They would all return to their lodges! Not one of them would remain to feed the Arkansas with their blood! And as Hungry Horse had prophesied, they would bring back not only their stolen ponies, but those of the Pawnees as well!

Four days later Standing Elk—as the most eloquent among them—rode ahead to the Comanche village to proclaim their great victory. When Hungry Horse and the rest of the war party drove the herd of ponies to the outskirts of the village, they were met by a laughing, cheering crowd of Comanches. It was close to dusk and already a great bonfire was leaping skyward in the center of the village. Jed felt eager hands pulling him from his pony and realized that this night the drums of victory would beat incessantly. Exhausted though he was, he would get no sleep.

When morning came and the warriors were

finally allowed to collapse in their lodges, Jed
was given one of Buffalo Hump's finest buffalo
robes to sleep on and an honored place in the old
chief's lodge.

By this sign did Buffalo Hump acknowledge
with pride his new son.

And no longer was Jed to be known as Scowls-
at-the-People. Hungry Horse and Standing Elk
wasted no time describing Jed's awesome, swooping destructiveness as he led them from the timber to do battle with the Pawnees. And when the
tale of Jed's awesome ferocity was completed,
Little Fox insisted that Jed had reminded him of
a swift and terrible bird of prey swooping out of
the night to devour his enemies.

From that moment on, Jed had a new name
among the Kwahadi Comanches. Henceforth he
was to be known as Golden Hawk.

—4—

Two Horns' war party returned to the village a
week later, driving before them two mule-driven
wagons and a large herd of blooded horses. Four
of the braves returned slung over their ponies.
As the bodies of these slain warriors were deposited before their lodges, the air was rent with the
fierce cries and frantic keening of old men and
women, sons and daughters, and the women of
the dead warriors. The old men cut off their
hair, while the women, insane with grief, took
up their knives and slashed at their breasts or
chopped off fingers.

Dusk fell, and before long the shrill cries of
bereavement faded. The gathering darkness came
alive then with the beat of drums and the high
piping of reed flutes as the celebration in honor
of those warriors who had returned safely took
hold. Standing close about the roaring fire, re-

splendent in their war gear, the warriors related their bloody exploits.

They had much to recount. Two Horns had taken them deep into Texas, where they captured more than twenty fleet horses. On their return, they had intercepted a supply train on its way from Independence to Fort Worth. The Missouri teamsters had fought fiercely and accounted for the four dead Comanches. Afterward, the teamsters had died slowly for their pains, and the war party had come away with two of the wagons intact, eight tough Missouri mules still in their traces.

Yet, even after this great victory, the war party hadn't been content. Coming upon two ranch houses in a lush river valley, they attacked. When they rode off, both ranch houses were in flames, fresh scalps hung from their lances, and they had taken six captives: four young women and two children. The children were brother and sister aged six and eight, ideal ages for adoption into the band. Three of the four women would make excellent slaves. The fourth would have to be killed. She had been pregnant when she was captured, and her treatment on the long trek back had left her wild and useless, gibbering one moment, laughing the next. She had apparently lost her mind.

The distribution of loot began. Into the darkness behind Buffalo Hump's lodge, Jed retreated to watch. He wanted none of the goods.

Two Horns and members of his raiding party pulled from one of the wagons long pine boxes

and casks of gunpowder. Shattering the boxes
with single strokes of his battle ax, Two Horns
reached in and handed out new percussion breech-
loading carbines, the bright polish of their bar-
rels gleaming in the leaping firelight. Proudly,
grandly, like fathers bestowing gifts on their
children, Two Horns and the other members
of his war party gave all the carbines away,
then distributed the gunpowder and lead, the
bullet molds and knives. They handed these
treasures out almost casually, and the generosity
of Two Horns and his war party stunned every-
body.

The first wagon gutted, Two Horns indicated
the second wagon with an imperious wave and
announced to those crowding around that they
might take from it whatever provisions they
needed. With a howl of delight the braves and
their women clambered into the wagon. Inside,
they found sacks of beans, casks of sugar, molas-
ses, flour, coffee, and tobacco. Ripping open the
boxes and casks, they filled the air with cries of
astonishment as they pulled forth each new pro-
vision or miracle of white men's manufacture.
They clambered down hugging to them brass spit-
toons, enameled chamberpots, mirrors, beads, silver ladling spoons, trunks of clothing, bolts of
cloth.

Before long, the braves were dancing around
the fire, dressed in top hats and morning coats,
shooting off their new carbines. Some wore bright
ribbons in their hair; others had on ladies' bon-
nets; a few tied silk scarves around their necks.

Soon the younger women of the tribe got caught up in the frenzy and joined the men in their wild dancing. Jugs of whiskey had been found in the second wagon, and despite the Comanches' misgivings about the stupid water, as they called it, the jugs were being passed around. A lopsided moon rode high into the night sky. The revelry increased to a fierce, savage intensity. All about him Jed saw the young women dragging the men into the shadows, while from all sides came the sounds of retching warriors.

The spectacle sickened Jed. He knew the cost of this drunken revelry. The lives and fortunes of innocent men, women, and children. The death of four brave Comanche warriors. He wanted no part of the celebration. He turned his back on it and disappeared into the shadows, wading across the stream to his own hut.

He sat cross-legged in the darkness outside its entrance. Sleep was impossible. The frenzied beating of the drums came clearly to him from across the stream, and he found himself thinking of the captives Two Horns had brought back. Over the years, Jed had seen many captives dragged into the village, many in far worse condition than those who had arrived today.

The captives were very badly treated, and Jed had had a hard time preventing himself from intervening.

This occasion—though he was now the adopted son of Buffalo Hump and an honored member of the Antelope band—was no exception. He still seethed inwardly at the Comanches' treatment

of their captives. The scene earlier, when Two
Horns presented the white women captives to
the families of the slain warriors, had been especially difficult for Jed to watch.

The two captive white children, wild-eyed
and shuddering with terror, had been snatched
up eagerly by a childless Comanche couple. By
now, Jed had no doubt, the adoptive parents had
torn off what remained of the children's shoes
and clothing and replaced them with buckskin
leggings and moccasins. Soon the brother and
sister would eagerly adopt Comanche ways. It
wouldn't take long before they became more
Comanche than the Comanches themselves.

A soft voice beside Jed interrupted his thoughts.
"Alonzo told me you were here."

He turned quickly. Raven Woman was standing in the shadows. Taken by surprise, Jed could
only shrug. "I am not hiding," he told her.

"Perhaps. But Buffalo Hump is angry."

"At me—or at Hank-of-hair?"

"At you. He says you have shamed him. Though
he has adopted you, you are not a true Comanche."

Jed wasn't surprised. It was a severe breach of
custom for him not to participate in this celebration for the returning warriors. But it couldn't
be helped. Jed would die before he participated
in the celebration of a war party that boasted
Two Horns as its leader. Or brought back white
captives.

"Tell me, Raven Woman. Why do you not join
in the celebration? Are *you* not a true Comanche?"

She stepped closer, then dropped beside him,

her large, liquid eyes regarding him solemnly.
"The braves drink the stupid water. I see familiar faces, but I do not recognize them. A different brave looks out at me. The stench of vomit
clings to them." She smiled and leaned closer.
"You do not stink of vomit."

"Tell me. Does old Buffalo Hump drink the
stupid water?"

"Yes, even he."

"And Two Horns?"

"Like you, he remains aloof. I think he looks
for you."

"He will find me soon enough."

"That is what he says."

"You should go. There may be trouble."

She shrugged and smiled impishly. "I do not
care. Besides, I look in your eyes and I see that
you want me. So I wait. But you do not approach
me. Is it true what they say—that Golden Hawk
only looks at women?"

He glanced away from her. "I am a man like
any other."

"No. You are not like any other. Buffalo Hump
is right. You are not a true Comanche. My mother,
she says so too." Raven Woman got up and, with
one quick glance back at him, ducked her head
and disappeared inside his hut.

When he had first became a herder of horses
for this Comanche band, many older Comanche
girls had sought him out. But none had truly
satisfied him. Only Raven Woman interested him.
In fact, she had been on his mind since the night

of his fight with Wolf Tracker and even more insistently since his return after the Pawnee raid.

He got up and followed Raven Woman inside.

She had lit his candle and was lying on his blanket, naked. As the flickering light played over her dusky figure, he caught his breath at sight of the dark splash of her pubic hair. It almost matched the sheen of the long, dark hair that spilled over her gleaming shoulders and coiled about her breasts. From head to toe, she was a deep, lustrous brown. Her breasts were large but firm, the nipples erect, waiting.

He quickly slipped out of his breechclout and lay down beside her. She embraced him and kissed him hungrily on the lips. He rolled eagerly onto her, his powerful erection seeking her pubis.

"No," she whispered fiercely, pulling her mouth from his. "Me on top. I want to ride you like a buffalo pony. Only it will be slow, Hawk. So slow!"

Suiting action to words, she pushed him over onto his back, suspended herself astride him, then lowered herself onto his erection with a mastery and gentleness that delighted him. Coming to rest, she wriggled her behind just a little and settled herself at least a couple of inches lower. He was completely engulfed by the moist, enclosing warmth of her.

With a sigh, she began to rock, slowly, very slowly at first, then increasing her pace almost imperceptibly. It was a revelation for him and bore no resemblance to the hurried couplings he had experienced with those other girls who'd come to him. As if from a great height, Raven Woman looked down at him, warmly. Giving him pleasure was delighting her as much as it did him. By now, her tempo has increased. Tiny beads of perspiration were showing on her upper lip and forehead, and she was beginning to pant slightly. Reaching up, he took both her breasts in his big hands and flicked at her nipples with his thumbs.

Jed himself was lost now in the sweet frenzy of it. Raven Woman rode him with increasing abandon, almost wildly, and still with infinite skill. Every downward thrust of her body seemed to meld them into one complete, passionate entity. Each time she rose along his shaft, he felt the panic of losing her until she plunged back down upon him and he was able to lift under her, meeting her thrust for thrust.

She moaned. He saw the pink edge of her tongue dart across her upper lip. Abruptly, she shuddered deeply, threw her head back, and closed her eyes, her face hardening into a fierce grimace of pleasure. He heard her gasping shriek, and then she was leaning forward, her breasts slamming onto his chest, her fists beating him about the shoulders as she continued to climax. He ignored her pounding fists, grabbed her firm buttocks with both hands, and rose into her again and again, astonished at the orgasms that exploded repeatedly from his groin.

At last their coupled fury subsided. He felt drained, empty— aware of a sweet, incredibly delicious languor. Laughing softly, Raven Woman rolled off him. He reached up and caressed her dark, lustrous hair, letting his hands become entangled in the thick, rich fullness of it. They were both acting like two children who had discovered a delightfully naughty way to spend an afternoon.

He had no idea how long they lay there, gazing into each other's eyes, but suddenly she bent and began to kiss his face, chest, arms, stomach, the hollow of his thigh. The feel of her lips was like a hot, moist flame. At first he wanted to tell her to pull back, relax, that she had wrung the last ounce from him. But it would have been a lie if he had, for her tongue worked an incredible magic on him. Soon he was not only erect again but reaching out hungrily, savagely to take her. Pulling her close, he swung astride her, intent on taking her now just as she had taken him.

"Ah-ee," she cried as he plunged deep within her. "Yes!"

She fastened her lips on his and flung her arms about his neck. Their tongues embraced. Jed was no longer conscious of her beneath him. He was now answering a deeper, wiser force, and he felt himself swept along in a swift, urgent wildness, not caring if he hurt her, intent only on reaching a distant crest. He slammed into her wildly, grunting, while she flung her head from side to side. Deep, guttural huffing sounds exploded from her straining throat. He found himself laughing finally, and nearing his climax, he flung his head back and howled. . . .

*   *   *

"I tell you what," Raven Woman said softly, entwining a lock of Jed's hair about her finger, "Buffalo Hump is right. You are not real Comanche."

"Why do you say that?"

"Because you do not make love like a Comanche."

Jed frowned, not sure of her meaning.

"Yes, it is so," Raven Woman insisted. She bent close to Jed and kissed him on his lips. "You do not get drunk and beat your woman when you make love. You do not go crazy and bite like an animal. You make love like my mother said the Spanish gentlemen make love: strong, fierce, like a tiger—but gentle!"

"Your mother remembers, does she?"

"Yes. She remembers how it was before the Comanche took her. And she tells me. Everything."

Jed said nothing.

Raven Woman leaned close. "But if you stay here in this village much longer, you will be like the other Comanches. Then maybe you will make love like a true Comanche—with your fists, and sometimes your teeth. That will be something," she cried, her eyes gleaming in anticipation.

"You think it will come to that, do you?"

"Already scalps fly from your scalp pole. Is that not so?"

Jed thought it wise not to reply. He saw Raven Woman in a new light. There was Spanish blood in her, yes. But she was like all those taken young by the Comanches—more of a Comanche than her captors, and eager to prove this. He would have to be careful with her, he realized with a pang. With Raven Woman he had hoped it might be different. But she was more Comanche than not.

He turned his head and looked out through the hut's opening. The eastern sky was growing lighter. The ceaseless drumming and the shrieking cries of celebration had stopped finally, and the village was silent. Not even the dogs were barking. Jed looked back at Raven Woman.

"You better return to your lodge."

She shrugged. "Why? No one will miss me. My father will be sick from the stupid water— and so will my mother. They will think only that I have found a warrior to comfort."

"You are not tired?"

"Yes. But I will sleep here. With you."

"Even though I am not a true Comanche."

She smiled quickly, her bright teeth gleaming in her dark face. "That is why I will stay. You will not get sick all over me. You will not raise your leg like a dog and piss instead of going outside. I will stay with you until you go on the raid."

"What raid?"

"The one Two Horns will make next month. To Mexico. He is taking Buffalo Hump with him. And he says you will go, too. Two Horns wants to see you take white scalp before he believes you can be trusted to follow the Comanche way."

"What else did he say, Raven Woman?"

"He heard a brave call you Golden Hawk. When he asked why that was your name now, the brave told him of your exploits with the Pawnee. Two Horns listened, then he shook his head. He did not think it proved a thing to kill a Pawnee."

"He said that, did he?"

"Yes. There is bad blood between you two, is that not so?"

"It is."

"Someday you will have to fight him. As you did Wolf Tracker."

"Go to sleep, Raven Woman."

She pulled the buffalo robe up over her bare shoulders and closed her eyes.

Jed watched her for a while, then rolled over, his mind racing. If what Raven Woman said was true, he would gladly join Two Horns' expedition. His wounds were all healed. He was ready now. And once he was deep in Mexico, he'd make his move.

Until then, he would have to be careful. Very careful.

—5—

Just as Raven Woman had told Jed, the Antelope band's raid into Mexico was led by Two Horns. Buffalo Hump served as trail chief, and Jed rode with his friend Alonzo at his side. The Mexican's role—together with the other slaves and younger Comanches brought along for this purpose—was to keep track of and guard the band's herd of fresh ponies during battle or on raids. This wasn't an insignificant responsibility. Loss of the Comanches' ponies would be a catastrophe. A Comanche afoot was a pitiful sight. Worse, he was helpless.

Most of the Antelope band's warriors made the journey, taking their women with them. Raven Woman had insisted on coming along also. Since the night of Two Horns' return, she had remained with Jed. Jed knew the advantages to be gained by doing so. In finally taking a woman of the band into his lodge, he was no longer an outsider.

Buffalo Hump was obviously pleased and made this known. Even Two Horns was forced to keep his own council concerning Jed, and the parents of Raven Woman made it known that expensive gifts wouldn't be required to purchase Raven Woman if Golden Hawk could distinguish himself against the Mexicans as he had against the Pawnees. It would be enough that Golden Hawk was at last one of the People and that his prowess in battle would reflect honor upon Raven Woman and her parents.

Under the bright Comanche moon they followed the Comanche trace that took them deep into Mexico. Once they were safely beyond the large, walled towns, they set up a camp on the side of a mountain and began their plunder of the countryside. Bands of young bucks rode off continually to raid isolated villages and haciendas. Jed, however, made no effort to join these small raiding parties.

This didn't go unnoticed. A few days after the band set up their mountain camp, Alonzo came to him, his face showing concern. He warned Jed there was talk among the other braves concerning him. It was being whispered that Golden Hawk was reluctant to take Mexican scalps. And now Two Horns was boasting to all who would listen that he had been right all along. Even Buffalo Hump was finding it difficult not to agree.

Jed listened to all this without comment. He expected as much. When Alonzo finished, he thanked him but showed no concern.

"My friend," Alonzo said anxiously, "you must

not hang back any longer. The talk I heard is filled with envy and hatred. Little Fox is the only brave who defends you."

Alonzo spoke with such agitation, his eye patch dislodged slightly. For an instant the torn empty socket where once his eye sat was revealed. Beside Jed, Raven Woman gasped and turned away.

Alonzo quickly shoved the eye patch up over the empty eye socket and bowed with mock apology to Raven Woman. "I am sorry if I have offended you, *señora*," he told her in impeccable Spanish. "I did not intend to do so."

In harsh Comanche, she responded, "You are a slave, Alonzo. And you shall remain one. Go back to the horses and turn your evil eye on the wolves that prowl about this mountain."

"Yes, *señora*," he replied, still addressing her with elaborate politeness. Then he reached out and took Jed's arm. "Be careful," he warned.

He disappeared into the night, heading back to his post in the canyon where the horse herd was being kept. Jed was angry with Raven Woman for speaking as she had to Alonzo, but kept from chiding her. He knew the woman was jealous of his friendship with the bent little man. To her it seemed abnormal, and she hadn't hesitated to tell him this.

"Well?" Raven Woman demanded, peering at him in the manner of a woman already married to him. "You heard what Saddle Maker said. It is true. I have heard the same talk. The other women look at me and laugh behind their hands. When are you going to ride out and bring back Mexican scalps?"

"I will go out at once and kill many Mexicans," Jed told her. "Very many. Then I will bring back their scalps and testicles in a sack and empty them out over Two Horns' head."

"That is foolish talk," Raven Woman cried, alarmed.

Jed looked at her and smiled. "I was not serious," he told her. "But do you think anything less will satisfy Two Horns?"

"Listen! Two Horns will be leading a large raid upon a village south of here. If you join that raid, you will have the chance to show him what a fine warrior you are—as you were against the Pawnees."

"When will the raid leave?"

"Tonight."

Jed looked at her with amusement. She and the other women of the band knew more of what was going on than did the warriors themselves.

"How far is this place?"

"A night's ride. The village has a wall, but it is not a high wall, and there is a large gateway that has no gate. There are many horses in their corrals. There is also a school and a church. Lame Deer's woman is sure there will be many young children for the taking."

Jed nodded grimly. This was what he had been waiting for. "I will go on this raid," he told Raven Woman. "And not a Comanche will doubt my courage again."

Raven Woman smiled in relief. She didn't want

to be known as Golden Hawk's woman—not if he was a coward. When Jed saw the relief on her face, he turned away from her and left the lodge.

He was sorry he couldn't warn her of his intentions, for she would suffer grievous shame on his account before long. But if he told her, he knew where she'd go with the information: straight to Two Horns.

Only Alonzo knew what Jed planned—just as Jed knew what Alonzo would soon do.

Jed found Alonzo sitting on a ledge above the horse herd, his small, bent body covered by a buffalo blanket, his sombrero pulled down over his face. For a moment Jed thought Alonzo might be asleep. Abruptly, the Mexican turned, and Jed saw the muzzle of the ancient rifle he was holding, the moonlight glinting off its long barrel.

"Ah, my friend," Alonzo said in Spanish, "it is you."

The two men had often talked of this moment. Like Jed, Alonzo had been waiting for just the right opportunity. Now, during this raid deep into his people's country, he was ready to break free of the Antelope band and return to his people.

"Two Horns is leading a large raiding party to a village south of here," Jed said. "This would be a good time for you to leave."

"Yes, I was thinking the same thing. I am glad you have come. Now I can say good-bye to my friend from Kentucky."

"Do you have what you need?"

Alonzo twisted his head slightly so as to catch

Jed fully with his one eye. "I have venison, freshly jerked. The saddle I have fashioned is light and sturdy. And the pony I have chosen is a favorite of Two Horns. While he rides south, I will ride east." His teeth flashed in his dark face. "On his pony."

"Be careful."

"I will."

The Mexican stood up and opened his arms to Jed. Jed stepped into them and embraced the small powerful figure. Together they had endured much. Through the fires of their enslavement, they had forged a friendship that would last a lifetime. Both men felt this and did not need to speak of it. Jed stepped back and placed his hand genty on Alonzo's shoulder.

"We will meet again," he said.

"If not in this world, then surely in the next. Good-bye, my friend, and good luck. May God be with you."

"And may God go with you, Alonzo."

Jed could say no more. He turned and moved off the ledge and headed back to the Comanche encampment.

They were only hours into the move south to the Mexican village when Jed saw Two Horns riding back along the column. As he rode, the war chief carried something pale and bulky in his right arm. When he drew abreast of Jed, Two Horns pulled his pony around so as to keep pace with him. Jed still couldn't see what Two Horns was carrying. But the war chief seemed greatly pleased, his dark eyes gleaming in the moonlight. He was like a returning warrior eager to recount his latest coup.

"Soon Golden Hawk will be killing Mexicans," Two Horns remarked in Comanche to Jed.

"Yes," replied Jed.

"After this raid I think we will swing to the northeast and raid the *tejanos*."

Jed shrugged, as if he felt this was to be expected.

"And we will take many captives," Two Horns went on. "White women and white girls and young boys."

"Yes," Jed said, keeping his eyes straight ahead now. For some reason Two Horns had chosen this moment to goad him into anger.

"But first," said Two Horns, "we kill the Mexicans."

This time Jed said nothing as he continued to look straight ahead at the long line of Comanches riding through the night.

Two Horns said, "How many will you kill, Golden Hawk?"

Jed shrugged. "How can I say that?"

"If you cannot say, then think on this, Golden Hawk."

As he spoke, he thrust at Jed what he had been carrying. It was Alonzo's crumpled sombrero. In the crown's pocket sat Alonzo's bloody, severed head, his face turned to Jed, his one eye staring wildly at him. Two Horns flung away the sombrero. The straw hat flew off into the night. Alonzo's head struck the ground and vanished.

Jed looked away from the war chief. "It is of no concern to me," he said.

"The Golden Hawk speaks wisely," Two Horns said. "This slave was a thief. He was caught riding off on one of my finest ponies."

"Then he was a fool."

"Yes. And now we will kill more Mexicans."

Jed said, "And I will join you."

Two Horns looked closely at Jed. The Comanche chief was obviously stymied. He had shown Alonzo's head to Jed in order to goad him into a fury that would reveal his true loyalties. But it hadn't worked. Abruptly Two Horns dug his heels into his pony and vanished into the night ahead of the column. Jed rode on, aware of a sense of loss so great he felt numb all over.

The only thing alive in him was rage.

The sweltering air of midday was filled with the screams of maimed and dying men, women, and children, and the high, soul-shiveling war cry of the Comanches. Like ants fleeing a stomped hill, the Mexican villagers were running in every direction, offering little resistance as the Comanches rode through their midst, striking out at will, killing indiscriminately with their battle axes or lances, or loosing their arrows in a rapid fire so deadly there was no escape.

In the front rank was Two Horns. Behind him came Hungry Horse and Standing Elk. Jed was in the rear, swinging his battle ax as he defended himself against the few Mexicans who rushed at him with shovels and other crude weapons. But

Jed wasn't interested in killing Mexicans. It was Two Horns he was after.

Jed was trying to keep the war chief in sight when he felt something powerful strike his pony. The pony screamed and lifted on its hind legs, nearly throwing Jed. Glancing back, Jed saw an old Mexican with a meat cleaver in his right hand slashing wildly at his pony's back. As the pony, whinnying in pain and terror, finally collapsed under the murderous blows, Jed leapt clear and bore the old man to the ground beneath him. Twisting the cleaver out of the Mexican's hand, Jed used the back of it to club the old man senseless—and keep him out of further trouble.

Regaining his feet, he was just in time to meet the charge of another desperate Mexican who slammed into him and drove him back against the wall of the church. All the Mexican had for a weapon was an old cap-and-ball pistol. Pressing its muzzle into Jed's gut, the Mexican pulled the trigger. The ancient firearm misfired. Grabbing the pistol's barrel, Jed twisted the pistol out of the Mexican's grasp and swung it like a club. He caught the fellow on the side of his head. The Mexican's big hat flew off as he sagged crookedly to the ground.

Jed stepped back. He had no intention of killing the Mexican. But a mounted warrior, screaming like an eagle, swept past. Leaning far over, the warrior drove his battle ax through the Mexican's skull. Jed's thigh was covered instantly with a fine spray of brain fragments and bone shards.

Furious, Jed glanced up. It was Standing Elk

who had come to his assistance. Wheeling his pony about Jed, the Comanche warrior claimed a coup, pointing to Jed for later confirmation. Then he turned his pony sharply and took after a fleeing woman. She was dragging two small children after her, heading for the rear of the adobe schoolhouse. With a delighted cry Standing Elk jumped from his pony and raced after her on foot.

Jed followed.

He turned the corner of the schoolhouse in time to see Standing Elk bury his battle ax in the woman's back. Then Standing Elk leapt over her crumpling body and snatched up the boy and girl by their hair. Spinning about, he caught sight of Jed. Grinning, he displayed the terrified children to Jed as he would have two chickens he had just stolen. Then he flung his head back and laughed in triumph.

Jed didn't laugh. Instead, he reached back to his sheathed knife and sent it at Standing Elk. The warrior's laughter was cut short. Dropping the two children, he sagged to the ground, the knife hilt protruding from his chest. Striding over, Jed kicked the dead Comanche over onto his back and withdrew his knife. Then he turned to the two children. They were still sprawled on the ground where they had fallen when Standing Elk dropped them. Too terrified to move, they could only stare up at Jed.

"Vamoose," Jed told them in Spanish. "Get out of here!"

They didn't have to be told twice. Scrambling

to their feet, they raced off, leaving their dead mother sprawled facedown in the dirt.

That was when Jed caught sight again of Two Horns. He and Coyote Piss were chasing two nuns up the alley leading to the church. Their faces distorted with terror, the nuns ducked into the church. Leaping from their ponies, Two Horns and Coyote Piss raced in after them.

Jed darted across the alley that cut between the church and the schoolhouse and ducked into the church's rear entrance. Inside, he found himself in a short hallway, a curtained doorway to his left, a stairway to his right. Pausing in the sudden, cool darkness to get his bearings, Jed heard faintly, through the church's thick walls, the high-pitched screams of the Mexicans outside still fleeing their savage tormentors. He was eavesdropping on hell, Jed realized.

From the church nave came muffled screams, followed by the sound of a scuffle, then more screams, sharper this time, and clearer. Two Horns and Coyote Piss had finally overtaken the nuns. Pushing aside the curtained doorway, Jed stepped into the nave and saw Two Horns and Coyote Piss struggling with the two nuns near the church entry. They were surrounded by candles glowing in colored glasses.

As suddenly as they began, the nuns stopped screaming. Struggling now with grim, silent resolve, they were saving all their energy to fend off their attackers. With equal resolve, the two Comanches quickly ripped off their habits.

In the dim candlelight, the nuns' closely shorn

heads seemed achingly pathetic to Jed. Battle ax in hand, he hurried through the cool darkness toward the struggling couples. Two Horns flung the nun he was struggling with to the floor and began kicking her viciously into submission. The other nun broke away from Coyote Piss and raced down an aisle, the same aisle up which Jed was moving.

When she saw Jed, she screamed in despair and halted, flinging up her arm to protect her from this new attacker. At the same moment, Coyote Piss, tired of running after her, loosed an arrow into the nun's back. Her face slack in shock, the nun staggered past Jed, then collapsed facedown in front of the altar. One hand reached up for it. But it was too far. She crawled a few feet farther and reached up again. This time she was able to grasp the rail. She was still clinging to it when she died.

Coyote Piss pushed rudely past Jed and looked down in disgust at the dead nun. Then he turned back around to face Jed. "Ho," he cried. "Is this where the Golden Hawk hides? In the white eyes' church?"

Jed calmly ignored the question and blocked the Comanche's path.

"Get out of my way," said Coyote Piss. "I will join Two Horns. He has one still alive."

Coyote Piss started toward him. Jed didn't stand aside.

Seeing this, Coyote Piss's face grew wary. He stopped. "What is the matter, Golden Hawk? Do you not like what we do here?"

"No."

"Two Horns is right. You have the heart of a white eyes, not that of a true Comanche."

Jed smiled then, a cold, brilliant smile. "Yes, you pinch of skunk shit, I have the heart—and the soul—of a white eyes. I always have. Nothing you or your people could do would ever change that."

Jed's words were a challenge Coyote Piss couldn't ignore. The Comanche sprang at Jed, a wild, exultant cry breaking from his throat as he swung his battle ax. Jed used his own to parry the thrust. But the force of the collision caused both axes to be torn from their hands.

With a low snarl, like that of a wolf whose jaws have closed on his prey, Coyote Piss flung himself at Jed, rocking him back. The Comanche's finger encircled Jed's throat. Jed clawed at the viselike fingers, then reached back for his knife. With one swift downward thrust, he buried his knife between the Comanche's shoulder blades. Coyote Piss gasped, but refused to let go of Jed's neck. Jed pulled his knife free, then plunged it down into Coyote Piss's back a second time. Then a third. The Comanche released his grip on Jed's neck and slumped heavily to the floor.

His throat felt scalded, and it took a moment for Jed's senses to clear. He picked up his battle ax then and hurried up the aisle to where Two Horns, his bison headdress still fixed solidly on his head, was busily raping the nun. She lay beneath him, unconscious. Two Horns had beaten her so severely that the welts and bruises were already showing clearly in the candles' dim, flickering light. As he rutted, Two Horns' knees dug into the floor alongside the nun's pale thighs while his fingers clutched at the soft flesh of her shoulders. So intent was he on reaching a climax he paid no attention to Jed's approach.

Jed reached down and with one hand yanked the Comanche up off the nun, then flung him violently aside. The startled war chief stumbled back until he came to a halt against the adobe wall. In his eagerness to take the nun, he had flung off his breechclout. Crouched against the wall with his glistening penis still erect, his medicine bag dangling in his crotch like a third testicle, Two Horns resembled a grotesque horned dwarf.

But this confrontation was what Two Horns had always wanted. With an eager cry, he swept his battle ax up off the floor where he had put it, and rushed Jed. Jed ducked aside, then swung with his ax and caught Two Horns solidly in the chest. The steel blade cut a long shallow wound in his chest.

Two Horns shook it off and charged Jed, driving him violently back. Lights exploded deep in Jed's skull as the back of his head struck the wall. With an eager snarl, Two Horns slammed the handle of his war club lengthwise across Jed's throat. Jed dropped his tomahawk and grabbed the ax handle with both hands. Twisting to one side, he managed to keep Two Horns from crushing his Adam's apple. Then he kicked up viciously, catching the naked warrior in the crotch.

Two Horns gasped and bent forward, one hand clutching at his groin. Jed brought up his other knee, slamming Two Horns full in the face, driving him up and backward.

His gimpy leg gave way under him, but he recovered swiftly and managed to take a powerful swipe at Jed. The blade of his ax sank into Jed's left side. Jed yanked himself back. So deep had the ax blade sunk that his action was enough to wrench the bloody handle out of Two Horns' grasp.

The Comanche drew his long skinning knife and charged. Ripping the battle ax out of his side, Jed swung it high over his head and brought it down in a straight, murderous arc. Two Horns was intent only on burying his knife into Jed's gut. The battle ax struck between the bison horns, cut the headdress neatly in half, then sliced through the Comanche's skull clear to the nape of his neck.

Jed dropped the ax and stepped back from the sagging war chief. A fountain of blood was erupting from the spot where his head should have been. In that moment Jed hoped the Comanches were right—that in death this was how Two Horns would enter the Happy Hunting Grounds: with his skull split open like the two halves of a walnut.

Jed heard a gasp behind him. He turned. The nun was sitting up, staring at the bloody figure on the floor in front of her. Then she glanced up at Jed. Stark horror swam in her eyes. Hauling her upright, Jed told her in Spanish to flee—and quickly. The nun snatched up what remained of her habit and raced down the aisle, disappearing behind a curtain. Jed heard the sound of her footsteps racing into a hidden loft somewhere.

He looked back down at the dead Comanche chief, thinking bitterly of Alonzo. Jed had hoped that the death of Two Horns would ease somewhat the pain he felt. But gazing down at what was left of his old enemy, he found it helped a little—but only a little.

He turned then and hurried to the rear of the church. Stepping through the doorway, he caught sight of Two Horns' pony waiting patiently in the hot sun, the Hawken rifle that had belonged to Jed's father resting in its rawhide sling. He had almost reached the pony when he realized he was a bit light-headed. He looked down and saw that his entire left side and thigh were covered with a heavy mantle of blood, the flow coming from that deep wound in his side.

At that moment a small band of warriors with Buffalo Hump and Lame Deer in the lead swept around the corner of the church.

"Golden Hawk," Buffalo Hump called to him, "where is Two Horns?"

"He is dead," Jed replied.

The Comanches came to a sudden, confused halt. If true, this was disastrous news, an omen evil enough to jeopardize the entire expedition. And Jed knew this. Only very bad medicine could come from the death of one of their most successful leaders.

"Where?" Lame Deer cried.

"Inside the church," Jed said, "where I left him!"

Jed ignored the sharp, searing pain in his left side and swung up onto the pony's back. Then he uttered a high, cutting Comanche war cry and charged straight for the stunned warriors. Lame Deer and the others scattered. But not Buffalo Hump. The old warrior stood his ground and flung up his lance.

Lifting his father's rifle from its sling, Jed rode straight at the old chief and parried the lance easily with the rifle's long barrel. Buffalo Hump went sprawling backward into the dust. Sweeping on past him, Jed kept on around the church. A moment later he left behind the ravaged Mexican village with its burning buildings and the bloody, mutilated bodies and charged at full gallop out through the gate, heading north.

What he needed first was to find shelter where he could wash off this hated war paint and then somehow gain a white man's costume. He was plunging back into his old world from which he had been snatched so cruelly ten years earlier. But he couldn't do so as a breechclouted Comanche warrior in full war regalia.

The question was, could he do it at all?

—6—

At the first stream he came to, Jed washed off his war paint and did what he could to clean out the deep gash in his side. He bound it with a strip he tore from the skirt of his breechclout. Then he rode on through the night and well into the next day until he reached a small Mexican hacienda. There he traded Two Horns' exhausted pony for a fine, blooded black. Considering himself lucky to escape with his scalp, the Mexican cattleman made the deal eagerly, his wife and children peering out anxiously from the doorway of their tiny adobe ranch house at the powerful blond Comanche.

By the third day his wound was flaring painfully. That night he entered a small ranch house without knocking and slumped into a chair. He rested his rifle on the kitchen table and fixed the astonished woman of the place with his feverish blue eyes and spoke to her in Spanish.

"See to my wound, if you please, *señora*."

"Put away the rifle," she told him calmly. "You do not need it in this house."

Jed pulled the rifle off the table and lay it down on the floor beside his chair. That was satisfactory to the woman. She was tall, with dark eyes and black hair coiled into a crown on her head. He thought she was very beautiful.

As she turned to the stove to heat the water, the door was kicked open. Jed turned and saw her husband standing in the doorway, an ancient shotgun in his hand. It looked oiled and well-kept. Jed had no doubt that it was loaded and that the man knew how to use it.

"Put away the gun, my husband," said the woman as she poked the fire in her stove to life with a short poker. "This Indian is wounded."

"You Comanche?" the man asked, lowering his shotgun.

"No," Jed told him. "I am Jed Johnson from Kentucky. For many years I have lived with the Comanches. Now I have escaped."

The man and woman exchanged glances, then looked back at the astonishing golden-haired Indian who spoke fluent Spanish and announced that he hailed from Kentucky, wherever that was.

"I am Emiliano Sánchez," the man told Jed, stopping at the kitchen table and holding out his hand. "This is my wife, Primavera."

Jed took the hand and shook it.

As Primavera cleaned out his wound, Emiliano assisting, Jed told his story to them while their four children crowded eagerly into the small room to listen. Jed's Spanish, learned from Alonzo, was eloquent. It wasn't long before he had gained the sympathy of the Mexican family.

At last, his remarkable tale completed, the wound in his side bound tightly, an enormous fatigue fell over him. He tried to get to his feet, but couldn't. He sagged forward, so exhausted he nearly lost consciousness. The last thing he remembered was the gentleness with which Emiliano and his wife helped him over to a cot.

A few days later, weak but no longer disabled by his wound, Jed stepped up onto his black horse. This time he was wearing clothes that—if it were not for his shoulder-length golden hair—marked him as a Mexican caballero. From neighboring ranches had come various items of clothing: a black, flat-crowned sombrero, a muslin shirt, red bandanna, a buttonless leather vest, leather leggings, and riding boots that fit him almost perfectly. The boots were a gift from Emiliano and his wife, who stood now in front of their humble dwelling, their bright-eyed children standing close by them, watching Jed intently.

Gathering the reins in his hand, Jed made no effort to express what he felt. Despite his excellent Spanish, he didn't know how to say what was better left unsaid. And he knew that when he looked into the eyes of Emiliano and Primavera, they understood what he felt at that moment.

With a wave, he pulled his black around and set off, heading north once again.

* * *

Four days later, he crossed into New Mexico. In a week he was riding into the town of Concho. As he reached the wide, dusty square, he looked cautiously about him. This was the first white town he had visited since he left Kentucky as a boy of fourteen. The women of the place went about with their bodies hidden in long shawls; the men wore high-peaked sombreros and were dressed in white cotton shirts and loose-fitting baggy pants. For years Jed had heard the members of his Comanche band speak of this town as the chief trading post for Santiago, the Comanchero chief who dealt with the Antelope band. Even so, it had a sleepy, nondescript look about it.

Most of the squat adobe buildings faced onto a large plaza. The church diagonally across from the cantina was the tallest building. It totally dominated the town. The rest of the buildings were little more than mud huts. Their doorways were so low that even the Mexicans had to duck their heads to enter. Grass grew on the flat roofs, and the walls surrounding the houses were crumbling. Aside from the church, the most impressive building was a long, sprawling, single-story building, its portico held up by roughly hewn tree trunks. Each rafter beam sticking out from under the roofline looked like the barrel of a cannon. The main door was recessed and made of heavy planks several feet wide and many inches thick.

Aware that he was under observation, Jed dismounted in front of the town's only cantina and went inside. It reminded him dimly of the saloons he had passed hurriedly by in the Kentucky town where he'd been brought up. Here, he knew, stupid water was sold to the Mexicans, and the men of the town gathered.

He strode up to the barkeep. In perfect Spanish, he asked boldly for José Santiago. The barkeep, a slovenly fellow with a huge belly, was momentarily at a loss. He glanced quickly around. The men at the bar and those sitting at the tables were staring in some astonishment at Jed. The barkeep looked back at Jed and shrugged helplessly, as if he had never heard of the Comanchero trader.

Jed left the cantina, climbed back onto the black, and rode along the plaza until he found a livery stable. Dismounting, he led the black inside. Jed remembered dimly that in these white towns there were places for strangers to stay. Hotels, they were called. Or rooming houses. He asked the hostler where the town's hotel was.

The boy pointed out the hotel. It was farther along the plaza, a squat, two-floor adobe-and-mud building. Taking his Hawken and the rest of his gear with him, Jed crossed the plaza and entered the hotel.

At the desk a small, round woman turned the register so he could sign it. The register was a large, dusty ledger, thin blue lines crossing it. Scrawled signatures filled many of the lines. Jed carefully took the pen the woman handed him. It had been a long time since he had held such an instrument. He cleared his throat nervously, then reached far back into his youth for the hours of penmanship drill his teacher had forced him to endure and managed to sign his name. Finished, he looked down at his signature, Jed Johnson, and felt a quick elation. It was as if by this single act he had verified his freedom from the Comanche yoke he'd endured for so long.

The woman slapped the bell on the desk and a Mexican boy came running to take his gear and rifle. Jed followed him up the single flight of stairs to his room. The boy unlocked it and showed him in. Jed thanked him. The boy waited a moment, then left, somewhat crestfallen. Why, Jed had no idea. He locked the door, kicked off his boots, and threw himself wearily down onto the bed.

He was asleep almost instantly.

It was dark when he awoke, and he was ravenous. He pulled his boots back on and went downstairs. The smell of food took him across the plaza to a small restaurant. It was little more than a large room with a beamed ceiling, the kitchen in a smaller room at the back.

He found a table and studied the menu curiously. He hadn't read from a printed page in years, and much of the food listed was foreign to his Comanche-acquired tastes. He handed the menu back to the waitress and ordered a steak. When it came, it was garnished with fried onions and mushrooms and there was a side order of dark bread with plenty of lard to spread over it. A side dish of fried potatoes came with the meal, and mixed in them were sliced bits of peppers so hot it caused tiny beads of sweat to stand out on his forehead as he ate.

He ate greedily and washed the food down with two cups of steaming black coffee. The coffee was good and cleaned out his gut, wiping away any remaining fatigue. He leaned back in his chair, satisfied. It was the first good meal he had had in days.

The waitress was a small, dark girl with long pigtails down her back. When she saw he'd finished his coffee, she came over to his table and smiled and told him the bill. Jed smiled and shrugged and told her in Spanish that he couldn't pay.

He stood up and prepared to leave the place. Everyone in the tiny restaurant was watching him. The waitress turned nervously and said something to a woman standing by the kitchen door. The woman promptly vanished into the kitchen. A second later the Mexican who owned the place came out to deal with Jed. He was a short, powerfully built man whose dark face resembled that of an Apache.

In excellent Spanish, the owner asked politely, "How was your meal, *señor?*"

"Very good," Jed replied just as courteously.

"Then you must pay."

"I have no money."

"You cannot come in here and eat without paying."

"I was hungry."

The owner ran his hand through his thick black

hair in exasperation. He wore a perfumed oil in his hair that made Jed's stomach queasy. Jed looked about him. Suddenly he became aware of the looming closeness of the walls. Despite everything, it seemed, there was still some Comanche in him.

He turned and strode from the restaurant. The owner overtook Jed just as he reached the square.

"Son of a dog!" he told Jed. "You will pay for that meal!"

"I have no money, señor," Jed repeated patiently. "I am sorry. It was a fine meal. Thank you."

The restaurant owner's eyes narrowed. There was something strange, even unnerving, about Jed that warned him. For the first time, it seemed, he noted Jed's sun-darkened, rawboned face, the splash of blond hair that reached clear to his shoulders and the fierce, Comanche-like fire in his smoldering blue eyes. So well did this blond giant's shoulders fill out his jacket that its seams looked about ready to burst. This was a most unusual caballero, obviously. He evoked something wild and untamed that only for this moment wore the dress of a civilized man. The restaurant owner cleared his throat, now at a loss as to how to proceed.

"Well," he said uncertainly. "You say you have no money?"

"Correct, *señor*."

"Pay me when you get it then."

Jed smiled warmly. *"Gracias, señor."*

Turning on his heels, Jed crossed the square to

the cantina. He asked the barkeep for a bottle of whiskey and took it along with a glass to a table near the wall. Slumping into the wooden chair, he poured whiskey into his glass and pretended to sip it.

Before long, a steady stream of hard-bitten men began filing into the place. From their dress, Jed guessed each was a Comanchero. He'd seen enough of them pulling up outside his village over the years, their big wooden carts with their groaning wooden wheels piled high with beads and other trinkets for trade. These men never bought more than a single drink, tossing it down quickly, then with a single glance at Jed drifted back out.

Before long most of Santiago's Comancheros had gotten a pretty good look at the blond stranger who had ridden into Concho this afternoon and was looking for José Santiago. Jed's boldness—or outright foolhardiness—intrigued them. They were anxious to find out who he was and what his business might be with José Santiago.

Jed knew he was taking a calculated risk. But he had no choice. He'd decided to regard this New Mexican town as he would any Indian village. The best course when approaching a Comanche or a Kiowa encampment was to do so boldly, accept the village's hospitality, and then wait for the chief to summon you—if that was his wish. In this particular village, José Santiago was the chief.

Jed was waiting now for Santiago to summon him.

He waited patiently, careful to drink only a bit

of the whiskey in his glass. He'd need all his senses alert when the time came. He was unarmed, save for his throwing knife in its sheath at the back of his neck. He'd left his Hawken rifle behind in his hotel room. He knew he was playing a dangerous game here in the center of a Comanchero outpost, but any risk was worth taking to see Santiago and learn where the man had taken Jed's sister. Already too much time had been lost.

The cantina emptied out and the barkeep started placing chairs upon the tables. Jed watched this curious custom with some interest. When the barkeep came to his table, Jed understood. He stood up and stretched his tall, powerful figure like a big cat. It was time to leave, so he strode out through the batwing doors and halted on the cantina's low porch.

The desert night was cooling the town off fast. Disappointed that José Santiago hadn't sent for him, he started back to his hotel. As he crossed the head of an alley, he heard the sudden scurry of footsteps. He started to turn, but the three men fell on him with sudden, methodical thoroughness. Two grabbed his arms while the third stepped in front of him and dealt him a series of murderous blows about the head and face with the barrel of his revolver. Finally, Jed sagged forward, still in the grip of the two men. Then a fourth attacker appeared out of the alley, measured the blow carefully, and sank his fist deep into Jed's groin.

While he retched helplessly on the ground, the

four men finished him off with their boots. Darkness closed in around him and there was little he remembered after that—except for the sudden dampness of a cellar, followed by the stench of a filthy, unventilated cell as he was hurled into it. He was dimly aware of his hat being flung in after him and the sound of a heavy wooden door slamming shut, followed by the rasp of a bolt being rammed home.

Then he passed out completely.

He was stiff all over and shivering from the desert chill when he came to his senses. He looked up at the single small barred window above him. Stars winked in a black heaven. He reached back to see if he still had his knife sheathed behind his neck. It was still there. Too bad he'd had no chance to use it. But those four men had been too fast. He curled himself into a ball and went to sleep.

When he awoke again, a solid beam of light was pouring through the window. Sitting up, he felt his face. It was swollen in places and both cheekbones were sore to the touch. There was a gash on the side of his head, and his gut was still sore. But the beating hadn't killed him; he'd live. Inching back carefully, he braced himself against the damp cell wall.

Heavy footfalls sounded in the passageway outside his cell. The door was pulled open and a huge bear of a man was flung into the cell. The fellow slammed into the wall beside Jed, then sank to the floor. The heavy cell door slammed shut, the bolt shot home.

Jed looked at his new cellmate. This was a bear of a man. His shoulders were massive, his face covered with a wiry red beard streaked with gray, and his reddish hair, like Jed's, reached clear to his shoulders. His shirt was open, and Jed glimpsed a bright-red flannel undershirt. His fringed, buckskin jacket came to his knees. Tight, wrinkled leggings encased his legs, and on his feet he wore soft deerskin moccasins. Instead of a sombrero or wide-brimmed hat, he had on a fox-skin cap.

When the big man saw Jed's steady gaze, he grinned. "I couldn't pay for my supper, either," he told Jed in English.

Jed smiled. "Who are you?"

"Tom Fitz. My friends call me Big Tom Fitz."

Jed didn't respond with his own name or shake Tom Fitz's hand. That was a white man's habit, and Jed wasn't sure he liked it. Besides, he didn't know if he could trust this new cellmate of his. Or any white man, for that matter.

Big Tom Fitz asked, "You're the one runnin' from the Kwahadi, ain't you?"

"How do you know that?"

"Word travels fast in Comanchero country," Tom Fitz told him. "Truth is, two of them Comanches already been here looking for you."

Jed said nothing, waiting for the big man to go on.

"They was here less'n a week ago," Fitz went on. "I was in the cantina when they rode in.

They had hell in their eyes and brimstone in their bellies. Called you Golden Hawk, they did, and gave a pretty fair description of you—'cept for them Mexican duds you're wearin'."

"How were they called?"

"Lame Deer was one of them. I think the other was Hungry Horse."

"Yes. I know them."

"They palavered some with Santiago. Then he told his men to keep an eye out for you. From what I hear, he told them two Comanches that if he found you, he'd deliver you to them alive—if possible."

"And where is Santiago now?"

"Upstairs, chucklin', I imagine."

"Upstairs?"

"Sure. This here's his warehouse. He's got his living quarters on the second floor. I figure he's been watching you pretty careful since you rode in."

Jed rested his head back against the wall. He'd come to the right place. He'd found Santiago. But he had misjudged the shrewdness and tenacity of those warriors he'd left behind in Mexico. They had known that Jed's first move would be to go after his sister, and that meant finding the Comanchero chief who had taken her from the Antelope band.

And Jed had delivered himself meekly into Santiago's hands, riding in boldly and announcing just as boldly that it was José Santiago he sought. Already Santiago must have sent a rider after Lame Deer and Hungry Horse to tell them of Golden Hawk's capture.

"Hoss, you mind tellin' me why you want to see Santiago so bad?"

Jed told him only as much as he needed to know: that he had business with José Santiago, business of a personal nature.

"Personal business, hey? Well, I got personal business with that son of a bitch, too. How'd you like it if a little later we go on upstairs and wring that oily bastard's neck?"

"That won't be easy."

"You just leave that to Big Tom Fitz."

Jed studied Tom Fitz more closely. What manner of man was it, he wondered, who spoke so easily of escaping this cell and wringing the neck of the most powerful Comanchero chief in New Mexico?

Tom Fitz's face was burned almost black from the sun. His hazel eyes were quick, alert. His nose had been broken in several places, Jed noted, and a long, faint scar that ran from the ridge of his left eye clear to his jawline was nearly lost in the extensive wrinkling of his worn map of a face. Jed figured the man to be close to fifty.

"You're not a Comanchero?" he asked Tom Fitz.

The big fellow shook his head emphatically. "I'm a trapper—beaver mostly—but I'll take after any fur-bearin' critter that'll bring me a good price. I been in the mountains west of here the past winter, but it wasn't a good season for me. No, sir. This here country's near all trapped out,

I'm thinkin'. There ain't hardly no beaver or fox left."

"Too bad."

"Yep. Guess I'll be going north, come fall."

"If you get out of here."

"Hell," he exploded, laughing. "We won't have no trouble getting out of here. Ain't you caught on yet? After I saw them critters catch up to you outside the cantina, I fixed it so's they'd throw me in here with you."

"And how did you manage that?"

"Well, first off, I drank enough to lubricate my tonsils some, then stormed about and told the barkeep if you didn't have to pay for your drinks, there was no call for me to pay either. He called some of Santiago's men over. I dared them to lock me up like they locked you up. And after a little tussle, they tossed me in here."

"They could have thrown you into another cell."

"Once in a while, a man has to take a chance."

"Now you are trapped in here like I am. You're a fool, I think."

"You ain't been listenin', hoss. I told you. I made them throw me in here 'cause I ain't got no notion of stayin' put."

"You know of a way out of this cell?"

"Sure, hoss. Look."

Chuckling, Tom Fitz unbuckled his pants and reached down past his crotch and pulled forth a bowie. He tossed the knife over to Jed, who caught it deftly by the handle, then felt the blade with his thumb. Razor-sharp, the blade drew blood easily. Still grinning, the trapper took a large skinning knife from the inside of his other thigh.

"Well, now," he said, "I figure this should help some."

Jed glanced over at the doorframe, held the blade's tip lightly between his thumb and forefinger, and threw it. The knife flashed across the cell, the tip of the blade sinking deep into the doorsill. Its balance was excellent, almost as good as his own throwing knife.

"You handle that bowie pretty damn good," Tom Fitz noted happily as Jed walked over and pulled the knife out of the doorsill.

"I still don't understand," said Jed. "You don't know me. Why'd you get yourself thrown in here with me?"

"Simple, hoss. You want to see Santiago, and so do I. But he's flanked by an army of bodyguards—mean critters, every one of them. You met four of them last night. So I figured the best way to get close to him was to get thrown in here with you."

"You want to see Santiago, too?"

"You bet your hind blister I do."

"Why?"

"It's a long story, hoss."

"I'm not going anywhere."

With a shrug, Tom Fitz began his story. "I got caught in a blizzard last winter. It was a mean one and I got caught with no winter gear. I wasn't doin' so good. My feet was about froze when a couple of Santiago's Comancheros came along. Instead of helping me, they stole my plews and my horse, and left me for dead. That made me so mad, my feet warmed up considerable. A month ago, I told Santiago about it. He was all apologetic. Slapped me on the back and stood me for a bottle of whiskey, he did. Then he told me he'd make good on the pelts and see to the men responsible."

"And he crossed you?"

"Do bears shit in the woods? The son of a bitch turned me over to the same critters what stole my plews in the first place. It took five of them altogether, but they worked me over pretty good. After they got tired of that, they dragged me out of town with a riata looped around my neck, then dumped me into the river. It was a high bank and the waters was swift, but I managed to crawl ashore about a mile and a half downstream."

"You die hard."

"Reckon so. Anyway, I got back in time to see them two Comanches who was lookin' for you ride in. I kept out of sight until tonight. All the while I been tryin' to figure how best to get back at Santiago. I'd be real foolish to go after him alone. Then you showed up and announced it was Santiago you wanted to see. So, like I said, I figured maybe the two of us together could do what one of us alone couldn't."

"We both have knives. You think that's enough to get us out of here?"

"Sure. I got a plan."

"Let's hear it."

"Times like this," Tom Fitz explained, "it's

always best to keep things simple. So we'll just wait in here until dark, then make a lot of noise to get them guards to come runnin'. Once they pull open the cell door, we use our knives. Then we go upstairs and settle our business with Santiago. The Mexican girl I been hidin' out with has your black and mine waitin' for us in the alley back of this warehouse."

"There's gear in my hotel room—and a Hawken rifle."

"A damn pretty piece that is, too. I took care of it. Don't fret none. The rifle and your gear is on your horse, waitin',"

"Seems like you thought of everything."

"It ain't best to leave much to chance—not in this world."

Jed sat back down under the window and leaned his head back, the bowie held lightly in his right hand. Like Big Tom Fitz said, it was so simple it just might work. If he had to tie up with someone, Tom Fitz was sure as hell big enough to hold up his end and then some.

Jed closed his eyes, rested his head back, and slept as quickly and as soundly as if he were reclining on a bed of pine boughs back on the high plains.

A corner of the moon was visible through the window as Jed crouched in the far corner. Tom Fitz had just screamed. When there was no response, he screamed again and kicked the cell door. It was a fierce blow and shook rust from the hinges. Then he whooped. When there was no response to any of this, he called out to one of the guards he happened to know.

"Diego!"

When there was no response, he resumed pounding, repeatedly calling out the guard's name. He kept at it until at last they heard heavy feet tramping angrily up to the cell door. When the guard shot back the bolt and pulled open the door, Tom Fitz was sprawled facedown on the floor. A knife was apparently protruding from his neck.

"Mother of God," the guard cried out, charging into the cell.

He bent anxiously over Tom Fitz. Like a striking rattler, the trapper rolled over and, with one swift, upward lunge of his knife, ripped open the guard's stomach, from crotch to brisket. The man gasped and slumped to one side.

The guard in the doorway flung up his rifle. But Jed's bowie was already flashing through the air. Its blade sank into the man's chest, slicing neatly between his ribs to his heart. Already a dead man, the guard toppled into the cell.

But there was one more guard standing in the doorway.

Terrified, this fellow dropped his rifle, turned, and bolted down the corridor, his cries loud enough to alert every demon in hell. Jed raced down the windowless passage after him. The guard flung himself up a narrow flight of stairs at the end of it. Halfway up the stairs, Jed caught him from behind and spun him around. The guard kicked out desperately. Grabbing a fistful of the guard's hair, Jed brought the blade of his right palm down on the side of the guard's neck. Slumping, the fellow tumbled loosely past Jed down the stairs.

Jed caught movement on the landing above him. José Santiago was stepping through an open door. Dressed in black pants and a shimmering white silk shirt with ruffles at his throat, the Comanchero chief looked very civilized. A huge Walker Colt revolver gleamed in his right hand.

Santiago brought up the gun and cocked it. Reaching swiftly back, Jed flung his knife. The blade entered Santiago's right eye socket. Santiago staggered back. Jed leapt up the remaining stairs as the Comanchero chief thudded to the floor.

"Santiago," Jed cried urgently, kneeling beside him.

Blindly Santiago groped for the handle of the knife. Jed pulled the blade out of the man's eye. At once a thick rivulet of blood began to flow from the ravaged socket.

"Where's Annabelle?" Jed demanded. "Where's my sister? What chief did you leave her with?"

For a moment Santiago seemed about to tell Jed what he wanted to know. Then he reached up to the bleeding socket, a feeble attempt to stem the flow of blood.

"Go to hell," he rasped, smiling cruelly at Jed. Then he died.

Jed stood up, his mind reeling. What had he done? With José Santiago dead, he had no clue to find Annabelle. He'd have to search every Mountain Cheyenne band, perhaps even those plains tribes as far north as Blackfeet country.

Tom Fitz pounded up the stairs. He was holding in his right hand a revolver he must have taken from one of the guards. He picked Santiago's big revolver up off the landing and handed it to Jed. Then he looked down at the dead man.

"Looks like you did it for me, hoss."

"Damnit, Tom! I killed him before he could tell me anything!"

"Tell you what?"

"Which Cheyenne chief he sold my sister to."

"Your sister?"

"Yes!"

Tom Fitz took a quick, short step back and peered closely at Jed, seeing his blond hair and blue eyes for the first time.

"Hey! You be talkin' about that blond woman Santiago took from them Comanches out on the Staked Plains? She's *your* sister?"

"Yes. You mean you heard about her?"

"Hoss, I know almost as much about her as Santiago. He brought her back here from the Staked Plains instead of tradin' her off. But she gave him too much grief, so he gave up on her and brought her north to a band of Mountain Cheyennes. Last I heard he sold her to a chief for a mess of beaver pelts."

"Do you know who the chief is?"

"White Cloud."

"Do you know him?"

"We smoked the pipe more'n once these past years."

"Can you take me to him?"

"If we hurry up and haul our asses out of here."

Jed sheathed his throwing knife and stuck Santiago's big Walker Colt into his belt, then nudged Tom Fitz back down the stairs.

When they reached the foot of the stairs, three Comancheros materialized between them and the outside door. The closest one raised his Colt, but before he could pull the trigger, Big Tom smashed him on the head with the barrel of his revolver. Then he lifted him high over his head and flung him like an oversized doll at the two behind him. All three Comancheros went down in a bone-crunching heap. As they struggled to get back up, Big Tom waded through them, his flailing revolver knocking them senseless.

More Comancheros were coming down the stairs behind them. Jed moved back swiftly to wait beside the stairs. When the first man appeared, Jed clubbed him with the big Walker, crunching through the man's skull. As he collapsed headlong, the second one tripped over him, landing at Jed's feet. Jed recognized this one as the man who had punched him in the groin. Jed kicked him in the head once. The man cried out, then flipped over onto his back. He tried to get up, but couldn't as blood pulsed from his nostrils.

"Let's go, hoss," cried Tom Fitz, pulling Jed around.

They climbed over the prostrate bodies. A shot from the darkness behind them took a bite out of an overhead beam. Jed turned and fired twice, the big gun bucking powerfully in his hand. No more shots came at them, and a moment later they burst out through the cellar door, ducked through the gate and down the alley. The horses were waiting, the Mexican girl holding onto their bridles. Big Tom Fitz gave her a bear hug that made her cry out, then swung up onto his mount. Jed was already on the black.

As they galloped out of town, the moon ducked behind a dark raft of clouds. The black night swallowed them up.

—7—

Bent's Fort rose out of the prairie huge and impregnable, a mud fortress capable of beating off even the Comanche bands that raided this far north, or the southern Cheyenne who swept this far south. Beyond the fort, chalk cliffs and shoulders of rock thrust upward, while the fort itself, built atop a bench, commanded a view of the prairie for miles around.

As Jed and Tom Fitz rode closer, the heat waves shimmering between them, the tops of Cheyenne lodges began to appear. The hides covering them were the same buff color as the prairie, making them almost invisible. And then suddenly they were in full sight, more than twenty of them ranging along the fort's east wall. Past the fort, on the other side of the Arkansas River, an entire Cheyenne village had encamped on a stretch of low sand hills.

Indian ponies were tethered at one end of the

village. At sight of them Jed recalled a long, miserable servitude. Smoke rose in thin plumes from cooking fires. All this Jed saw through the haze rising up from the prairie. It was as if he were looking through a distorted pane of glass at another world.

Or back into an old nightmare.

"These here are Arapaho lodges, sure enough," remarked Tom Fitz.

They pulled up for a moment to look around at the ragged tepees and the blanket-wrapped Indians squatting in the fort's cool shadows. Jed felt a surge of contempt. Often the Antelope Comanches talked of these tame Indians—how they had surrendered everything that was good and free, including their wives and daughters, in order to trade buffalo robes for the white man's whiskey and army blankets. Jed agreed with his former captors. These Arapaho and Cheyenne were not worth saving from the white man. They had already given themselves to him without a struggle.

Jed felt a hand tugging on his left boot. He turned his head and looked down into the dissolute face of a Cheyenne. Behind him was a woman who could have been his wife. She looked pretty well beat up. Her face was discolored and some teeth were missing. The man had closed one hand about her wrist. She hung back, but his grip held her remorselessly.

"White man, here is my woman," the Indian cried. "You take her for five dollar gold. Here! She very good. Not sick!"

"How much?"

"Five dollar."

"That's the price of a jug of whiskey up here," explained Tom Fitz. "Looks like the poor son of a bitch's fresh out."

Jed looked at his woman. A Cheyenne, she was tall and might have been pretty if her face hadn't been so ravaged. The sight of her got mixed up in his mind with his anxiety for his sister—and suddenly he was filled with a terrible rage.

"Get away from me, you dog of a Cheyenne," Jed cried in fluent Comanche. "Get away or I will take your scalp and make you eat it raw."

The Cheyenne was stunned. The sound of the harsh, Comanche dialect—uttered as only a full-blooded Comanche could—shocked him. Even his woman cringed back at the harsh sound of it. They realized that, despite his dress, this big man with the enormous shoulders and blond hair was not truly a Mexican as he looked, but a Comanche, as dangerous and as bloodthirsty a foe as any that ravaged a plains Indian's lodge.

The Cheyenne fled, dragging his woman after him.

"You sure scared the shit out of that one," Tom Fitz remarked.

Jed said nothing. He was still too angry. They continued on to the fort's main entrance, the rage within him slowly simmering down.

The entrance to the fort faced north, away from the river. On top of a wide, cylindrical tower to the northeast Jed noticed the snout of an enormous cannon. Directly over the entry gates rose a watchtower and belfry. As the two men rode closer, two of the men clustered to one side of the gate with a delegation of blanketed Cheyennes banged with the stock of their rifles on the gate, then waved Jed and Tom Fitz on in to the fort. Slowly the heavy, iron-sheathed gates swung open, and the two men rode on through. The walls appeared to be at least three feet thick, and glancing up at the wall's height, Jed judged it to be as tall as three men standing on one another's shoulders.

The *placita* was huge, filled for the most part with traders and a few emigrants and their wagons, their frightened young ones clustered closely about them. Jed noted the soft faces of the white women and the bearded faces of their men. He saw, too, Indians, Mexicans, travelers dressed in eastern finery, and those few heavily bearded mountain men, who, like Big Tom Fitz beside him, favored fringed buckskin and moccasins.

What most impressed Jed about the fort itself were the rooms built along both sides of the courtyard, some rising two stories high. They were fronted by roofed verandas and balconies resting on sturdy beams. The rooms on the east wall were set aside for storerooms, the kitchen, dining hall, and shops. About three feet above the roofline a parapet had been constructed, with firing ports set into the wall. Off to his right, Jed heard a shout, followed by laughter. Men stood in groups, smoking their pipes or lifting bottles to their mouths. They were riding on through this crush very carefully, toward the south end of the courtyard, where the interior corrals and other storage rooms were placed.

The air was pungent with the rank smell of buffalo hides and beaver pelts from the storage sheds, and from the kitchen Jed could smell fresh bread cooking and meat roasting. And above it all hung the stench of sweaty, unwashed men and animals mixed in with the acrid stench of cooking fires burning beside wagons everywhere about the fort. Why, in all this heat, there was need for so many fires, Jed couldn't imagine.

They left their horses and gear in the livery stable. Tom Fitz appeared to know the stable boy—an old man with bent legs and poor vision— and introduced Jed to him. The old man peered through his dim lamps at Jed and nodded agreeably, then sent a long dagger of tobacco juice into a pile of hay beside him.

With Tom Fitz in the lead, they headed then for a grog shop, as Tom Fitz called it, to settle the dust in their stomachs.

A moment later they squeezed into a smoke-filled room. There were low tables and benches everywhere, and a small counter at the far end served as the bar.

Tom Fitz pulled up in front of the barkeep. He was a broad-beamed fellow with thin black hair plastered across the top of his skull. Tom Fitz smiled at the man and inquired of someone called Old Bill. The barkeep shrugged. He'd never heard of the man, he said. With a sigh, Tom Fitz ordered whiskey for himself and Jed, paying for the bottle with a silver coin.

They found a table in the rear and sat down. Tom Fitz poured. The whiskey sent a hot wallop down Jed's gullet, clear to his instep, and he felt better at once.

"Who's Old Bill?" he asked.

"A friend," Tom Fitz said. "The times are bad, hoss. When the likes of a man sech as Old Bill is forgotten, the world's done turned too far for my taste." He poured himself another shot and downed it like water.

"Was he a trapper, like you?"

"He was that, and more, was Old Bill. He was a preacher once. Reads Shakespeare now *and* the Bible. Smells worse'n a buffalo cow in heat, and he's hated alike by the Blackfeet and the Crow. Thought to see him here this time of the year. I'm thinkin' of moving north into Crow country to find a stream thick with beaver, come winter."

Jed nodded, curious. "Why do the Blackfeet hate him?"

"Well, sir, it's like this. Once he was in Blackfoot country settin' traps alone when he was set upon by three braves looking for his scalp, greasy and unlovely though it be. They sent two arrows into Bill's hide, but he scrambled out of the stream and vanished into the woods. Bill's a right big son of a bitch, but he can disappear any time he wants, like he just makes himself plumb invisible.

"So the Blackfeet give up on him. Bill pulled one arrowhead out of him easy enough, but the other one he had to cut out of his leg. Then Bill went after the Blackfeet. They'd took his rifle, Old Fetchem, you see."

"You mean that's what he called his rifle."

"Yep. And it was a good name for the thing, though I could never understand how he could hit anything with it, the way it wobbled when he aimed it."

Jed chuckled and leaned forward. "Go on," he urged. "Did he get the rifle back?"

"You just let me tell this," Tom Fitz said, grinning while he poured. "Old Bill found them easy enough, then trailed them for three days. But the Blackfeet kept themselves healthy with jerky and were light sleepers. On the fourth day they shot a buffalo with Bill's rifle. Old Bill was happy to see that. He knew they'd gorge themselves on the meat and entrails. They did, and slept as though they was dead."

Jed nodded. Tom Fitz was right. Many were the feasts he had witnessed among the Antelope. They were not pretty affairs. Indians didn't eat in moderation, just as it was impossible for them to drink in moderation.

"So Bill steals among the Blackfeet," Tom Fitz continued, "and he didn't act like no preacher. The first buck he slew by slitting his throat, clamping a hand over the Indian's mouth at the same time, so his breath hissed out softly, 'stead of comin' out in a scream. That buck's scalp taken, Bill stabbed the second Blackfoot. This one was lying on his stomach and Bill just pushed his face into the ground to keep him quiet. The third brave he waked up deliberate and kicked him in his bloated stomach. The Blackfoot ran off, screaming.

"And Bill had Old Fetchem back."

"Why did he let that last Blackfoot go?"

"He wanted them Blackfeet to think of him as one trapper they'd best leave alone. And he wanted the news to spread from campfire to campfire, so his fame would grow. A man with such powerful medicine might move among them people without fear of losing his scalp."

"Or," Jed pointed out, "it might make some young buck all that more eager to go after him."

"Yep, that's true. But so far Bill's had no more trouble from the Blackfeet. And the Pawnees and the Crows give him a wide berth."

A dark shadow fell over their table. The two men glanced up.

"Bill! You old son of a bitch," Tom Fitz cried.

The gaunt, pockmarked man pulled up a chair and lowered himself onto it dourly, his piercing blue eyes glancing curiously at Jed.

"We was just talkin' about you," said a pleased Tom Fitz. "That fool barkeep said he didn't know you."

"Biff was just funnin' you, hoss," Old Bill told him. "He's the one got word to me you was here."

Tom Fitz turned about in his chair. The barkeep was smiling, and he waved at Tom Fitz. Then Tom slapped Old Bill heartily on the back and poured him a glass of whiskey.

"Bill," he said, "this here's Jed Johnson. Me and him just broke out of Santiago's prison."

"José Santiago? That old Concho trader?"

"That's the one. But he won't be doing any more business with the Comanches. That right, Jed?"

Jed sipped his whiskey. "Not unless he sets up a trading post in hell."

"Thought I heard something from down there," Old Bill said, appraising Jed shrewdly. "Took his scalp, did you?"

"Didn't bother with it. Took his Walker Colt instead."

Old Bill grinned and reached out his gnarled hand. Jed forced himself to take it and return the solid grip and shake. Old Bill did indeed smell like a buffalo cow in heat and his greasy buckskins were filthy, but he looked to be someone who would make a fine friend and a deadly enemy. He was an inch or more over six feet, gaunt, with reddish hair—a man all muscle and sinew.

Old Bill glanced at Fitz. "Where you headed?"

"We're lookin' for a Cheyenne chief—White Cloud."

"What d'you want him for?"

"It's a long story." Tom Fitz looked across the table at Jed. "You want to tell him, Jed?"

Jed shrugged and told Old Bill what he already told Tom Fitz, including the fact of his having lived from the age of fourteen with the Antelope Comanches.

At the conclusion of his tale, Old Bill nodded sagely and said, "Well, you better get a move on. White Cloud ain't no help to that band, from what I hear. And you know how the Crows love to devil a band they figure is ripe for pluckin'."

Jed knew nothing of what the Crows loved, but he took it for granted that Old Bill did—and that Annabelle was in a precarious position if she were still subject to that war chief.

"We'll be pulling out tomorrow morning," Jed told him.

"You'd best change them fancy duds, then. You'll need something a mite heavier where you're goin'—buckskins, maybe."

"We was planning on doing just that," Tom Fitz admitted. "But first I got to see Bent. He owes me for a mule load of plews I left here a year ago for him to sell. Is he about?"

"Just left him. He's upstairs in his apartment."

Tom Fitz slapped down his empty whiskey glass and looked at Jed. "Let's go see Bent," he said. "Then we'll go see about getting ourselves outfitted proper."

The three men got up then and walked outside. Old Bill walked strangely. He staggered and weaved some, but made it to the door without incident and walked with them to the bottom of the outside stairway that led up to William Bent's apartment.

Fitz and Jed ascended the wooden steps to Bent's apartment. One knock and a sharp voice told them to come in. The builder of this amazing mud-and-adobe fort was seated behind his desk. The small, powerful-looking man, dressed in soft white deerskin shirt and leggings, took one look at Tom Fitz and hurried around his desk to greet him.

After Fitz introduced Jed, there was a moment or two of casual chatter, then Fitz told Bent why he had stopped up to see him. Immediately Bent opened his safe and took out a small pouch. As he put it down on a table alongside Tom Fitz, it chinked richly.

"It's been in there, Tom, for close to a year now," Bent told the mountain man. "I'm glad you're healthy enough to claim it."

"Thanks, Will," Tom Fitz said. "I didn't have no doubt it'd be here when I came for it."

"You still trappin' them flat tails?"

"Might as well, now that I got enough to oufit myself."

"Which way you headed?"

"North."

"Good idea. Beaver's runnin' out hereabouts. Might be you'll have better luck in Crow country. Some of them fresh mountain streams, I hear tell, are fairly brimmin' with the critters."

Tom Fitz nodded. "Been hearin' the same thing. Come tomorrow morning, that's where we're headin'."

"Movin' out pretty fast, ain't you?"

Tom Fitz shrugged.

"Thought you might stay awhile with Old Bill. Maybe between the three of us, we might get him to take a bath?"

"Wouldn't try sech a thing. Once we unwrapped them buckskins, why, Old Bill would melt like lard in a skillet."

Bent laughed. "Shrivel him right up, it would." Then he looked closely at both men. "You two leave some trouble behind?"

"Maybe."

"Thought so. I been hearin' strange things," Bent said.

"Like what?"

"José Santiago is dead."

"Well, I declare!" Tom Fitz winked broadly at Jed.

"I'm hearin' something else too. That maybe you and this young giant had something to do with it."

"Ordinarily I'd say pay no attention to rumors, Will, but maybe there's a mite more truth in this one than in most."

"I see." Bent smiled. "And that's why you're in a hurry to get on out of here."

"That's part of it."

"Then we'll leave it at that."

An hour later, in what passed for a tailor's shop at the fort, Jed was peering at his reflection in a long sliver of a mirror. He was pleased. Unlike the confining Mexican duds, the fringed buckskin jacket gave him plenty of room—in the shoulders especially. And it was light and cool against his skin. The jacket reached to his knees. His leggings were buckskin also, and his feet were covered with deerskin moccasins.

His discarded Mexican duds were folded neatly over the arms of the dark girl who had helped him undress in the back room before his bath.

She was watching him now with dark, gleaming eyes. There was Indian in her, he could tell, and also some Mexican. She reminded him of Raven Woman.

Tom Fitz had already given the store owner enough money to cover Jed's new outfit. He had also tried to get Old Bill to take a bath, but the man had paled at the thought, and to help him recover, Tom Fitz had left the shop and gone to the grog shop with him.

The store owner came over to see how Jed was doing. "That there looks mighty fine on you, mister."

"It feels good."

"That's the genuine article—not some cheap imitation manufactured in St. Louis."

Jed turned to the girl. He had heard the store owner refer to her as Consuelo. "Consuelo," he said, "take the clothes, clean them, and give them to a friend."

"Thank you, *Señor*."

Jed looked at the store owner. "Is Conseulo your daughter?"

The man was shocked. He was a white man clear through, Jed saw. The intimation that this dark, half-breed girl might be a relative didn't please him. At once Jed disliked the man.

He turned back to Consuelo. "Do you have a caballero to give these clothes to?"

She shook her head sadly. "But I take them. I know a young man who thinks he will marry me one day. He will be very happy to get these fine clothes."

"Let's go meet him," Jed said.

"But I must work."

Jed turned to the store owner, took out the small leather sack Tom Fitz had given him, and tossed two more silver dollars onto the counter. "Give the girl some time off," he told the man.

At sight of the silver coins, the store owner's eyebrows went up a notch. "Two dollars?" He seemed pleased at the deal.

"Yes."

"Take her all afternoon, if you want."

Jed smiled and left the store with Consuelo.

On his way to Consuelo's room, Jed noticed Tom Fitz examining four pack mules he was purchasing for the trip north. One look at Consuelo and Tom Fitz grinned.

"I figured this one'd get her hooks into you."

"They are not hooks, *señor,*" Consuelo replied, her dark face flaming.

"No harm meant," Tom Fitz told her hastily, and winked at Jed. He told him now would indeed be a good time for him to get his ashes hauled good and proper. Old Bill had found a couple of clean Indians, and as soon as he finished purchasing provisions, Old Bill would be bringing them up to his room.

"How in blazes can Old Bill tell if them Indians are clean?" Jed wanted to know.

"It's a gamble, I admit," Tom Fitz replied, grinning.

Then he nodded good-bye politely to Consuelo and went back to examining the mules. As Jed moved off, he called, "Get back here before dawn. I'll need a hand packin.' "

Jed assured him he would.

Consuelo's room was very small. It contained a cot and a single dresser, a small table and chair in one corner, and a frayed bamboo rug on the dirt floor. A candle sat on the dresser beside a tin cup and an earthen water jug. A fat chamberpot sat under the neatly made cot. The pounded dirt floor was swept clean. There was only one window, high on the wall. Blocked by the fortress's wall, however, it let very little light into the room.

Even so, Consuelo had managed to find a wild flower. Still bright with color, it sat in a thin earthen vase on the windowsill.

As she put down the clothes Jed had given her on top of her dresser, she explained to Jed that the young man she would give the clothes to worked in the stables nearby. She was certain he would be very grateful and anxious to meet his benefactor.

This speech finished, she turned to Jed, eyes glowing.

Jed's loins ached. They had since Consuelo had waited for him to hand her his clothes before stepping into the water she had heated for him. Later, she had come back and washed his hair, then scrubbed his back. During all that he had felt his need building—and from the flush on her face as she occasionally glimpsed his engorged member, the need was climbing within her as well.

"You give me little holiday," she said. "I must thank you."

"How would you do that?" he asked, smiling.

She opened her arms to him. He stepped closer. Her ruby lips parted. "Like this," she said, kissing him.

Her moist, pliant lips began to work on his at the same time as her swift fingers undressed him. He kicked off his boots. She pushed him back onto her cot, and he lifted his buttocks to help her strip off the remainder of his clothing. She felt his powerful, surging erection and released his lips, laughing softly.

Stepping back, she quickly flung off her blouse, then stepped out of her long skirt to stand naked before him. Her eyes gleamed with anticipation as she stared at his long, powerful body and the tentpole surging from his crotch. She allowed him a few seconds to drink in her wanton nakedness.

His eyes feasted on her magnificent breasts, so much larger than those of most Comanche women. They were very round, with nipples large and thrusting. His gaze moved down across the swell of her belly, a provocative, round little mound that dipped into the lush, bushy triangle of her pubis. Her thighs flared wondrously. She was bursting with ripeness.

With a tiny rush she was in his arms.

"But you are so big! You will not hurt me?"

"I will be careful," he assured her as he straddled her eagerly.

"But do not be too careful!"

Her body seemed on fire. His also. Words were useless now. He could only nod to her, so eager was he to proceed. It had been such a long time for him—and for her too, he hoped. Moving his hips carefully, he entered her with gentle firmness, then pressed home. He felt her inner muscles tighten about his shaft. She groaned with the pleasure of feeling him so deep inside her. The tempo of her breathing increased sharply, her lips parting slightly, tiny sounds of pleasure breaking from them.

He began to thrust faster. With a hiss of delight, she met each thrust, eagerly slamming her hips up against his. Jed increased his pace and found himself taking longer and longer strokes, each return searing deeper into her, causing her to grunt with pleasure as he touched bottom. He was surprised at his own control, determined to hold back until she'd been satisfied. She was trembling from head to foot now, her grunts turning to tiny, delighted cries. Then came a final, throaty cry as her body convulsed under him and her hips jerked wildly for a moment before she released her last gusty sigh and grew limp under him.

He was still erect, still keeping himself deep inside her, the warmth and tightness of her muff inflaming him.

"You have not come, Señor Jed?"

"I don't want this to end so soon. Are you ready for more?"

"Oh, *sí*," she cried.

With a swift, skillful movement she rolled him

over and suddenly she was atop him, her hands resting on his chest for balance. He grinned up at her. He felt her internal muscles gripping his erection with the force of a clenched fist. She began to move slowly up and down, her muscles gripping him even tighter. Then she started moving her pelvis astoundingly as he admired the view. Her nipples were turgid and her lovely breasts bobbed in rhythm with her rippling lower torso muscles as she moved in a way that no Comanche woman had ever moved.

His control was lessening. A fire was building in his crotch. The tip of his erection was on fire. With both hands he clasped the sides of her flaring hips and thrust her down onto him with a violence that caused her to gasp. Crying out softly, she increased her pace. He rose up under her like a volcano. There was no more control, no more turning back. He fired up into her like a cannon.

She screamed. It didn't matter that those in the next apartments could hear her. Then she screamed again.

"I come too," she gasped, collapsing weakly down against him, her nipples teasing his chest as her spasming muff went on milking him. He felt himself throbbing softly as he continued to ejaculate into her.

Consuelo laughed lightly and ran her hands through his hair, then gazed lovingly into his blue eyes. "That was so nice, Señor Jed. You are so big. I want to swallow all of you." She kissed him, her warm lips working him eagerly. "This some holiday for Consuelo. I hope it is good for you."

"It is good for me."

"Then we do it again?"

Jed laughed and thought about it. And the more he thought about it, the better he felt. Then he became aware that another part of his anatomy had been thinking about it as well. It had risen to attention once more.

Jed chuckled. "Yes," he told her, enclosing her in his arms and rolling gently over onto her. "We do it again."

Consuelo and Jed spent the night together. She learned not only that Jed was fluent in Spanish, but that Raven Woman had taught him a few interesting variations. She was delighted with their potential, and when Jed left her before dawn to help Tom Fitz load the pack mules, their parting was long and delicious.

—8—

Jed sensed the danger.

He was at least a mile from the camp he and Tom Fitz had set up in the lee of the mountain. It was late in the afternoon, and for the past two hours Jed had been setting beaver traps. Striding in and out of the water, he pulled the dugout behind him as he worked, his nostrils quivering to the wild abundance of the grass and wild flowers, only dimly aware of the huge mountain masses shouldering skyward on all sides of him and of the sun's heavy warmth on his shoulders. He liked these mountainous foothills; they were so unlike the dry, windswept high plains where he had spent so much of his young manhood.

But now he felt this sudden, inexplicable alarm. It came from deep within him, tightened his belly, and caused his nerve ends to tingle. No longer lulled by the steady, monotonous rhythm of his labor, he peered alertly about him, his senses keenly alive as he peered into the thick beech and pine that crowded both sides of the stream. The birds had gone silent, he noticed. Then came a sudden flutter of wings. Turning in the direction of that sound, he caught movement deep in the trees that crowded the riverbank.

He reached back into the dugout for his Hawken, then stepped onto the solid shore. The disturbance had been some distance away, at least fifty yards. Jed felt no alarm; he was confident of his prowess with the Hawken and knew it could stop anything within its range. Practicing with it a week earlier, he had hammered a nail into a tree at fifty yards, driving it deeper with each successive blow of his lead balls. The Hawken fired in an almost flat trajectory for distances over a hundred fifty yards, he had discovered. And once he had been able to shoot the branch out from under a sparrow at two hundred yards without harming the bird. With an ordinary powder charge, the slow twist of the barrel's rifling gave almost no recoil. Even with heavier charges than normal, the kick was hardly noticeable and would not affect the deadly accuracy of his shooting.

After ten long years, the rifle that once served Amos Johnson so well now served his son.

Jed heard a deep, painful gruff, and the hair on the back of his neck stood up. He caught the movement as something crashed to the forest floor. It was less than fifty yards away now. Then the grizzly burst into view on the far side of a small clearing. An arrow was protruding from its neck. It was in a blind rage, and charging directly for Jed.

Jed didn't hesitate. Stepping out from behind a pine, he raised the Hawken and squeezed off a shot—all in one swift, fluid movement. The lead ball crashed into the animal's chest.

The bear shambled to a sudden halt, momentarily confused. Then it reared up on its hind legs and roared. Jed ducked back behind the tree, but it was too late. The bear had sighted him. Heavy and cumbersome, its lumbering gait appeared slow to the eye, but it devoured the distance between it and Jed with startling swiftness. Jed poured powder down the rifle barrel and followed it with a lead ball. In a second the load was seated. He lifted the crescent-shaped butt of the stock to his shoulder. By this time the bear was less than twenty feet from him.

Jed saw the bloody smear on its shoulder around the arrow shaft's base and noted the maddened light in the miserable beast's eyes. The grizzly roared, revealing his teeth and blood-red gums. Jed aimed again for the chest and fired point-blank, knowing full well that there was no animal harder to bring down than a bear—and that one swipe of those broad, taloned paws could rip him open end to end.

The half-ounce ball of lead smashed into the bear's chest alongside the first one. The ball's impact caused the grizzly to stop a second, but it kept on, its pace slower now, its legs unsteady. For a good ten feet or more it staggered on. Then, with an unhappy, defiant roar, it collapsed facedown in the brush. Jed saw two arrows protruding from its back.

For a dead grizzly, he had come a long way.

Jed knelt beside the dead animal, noting its size with wonder. It must have stood close to eight feet on its hind legs. As the great carcass cooled, swarming multitudes of lice began fleeing it, their gleaming trail winding over the animal's gaping snout.

Jed broke off one of the arrows and examined it. It was Cheyenne, possibly belonging to a band of the Mountain Cheyenne, the tribe Jed and Tom Fitz had been searching for this past month. Jed reloaded the Hawken and started back the way the grizzly had come, moving carefully, aware that if a Cheyenne brave was ahead of him, he wouldn't know or care if Jed was friendly or not.

Jed sensed movement behind him—the crush of grass under a moccasined foot. Whirling, he met the Cheyenne's charge. The tomahawk slashed past Jed's head, its honed edge slashing a long rent in his buckskin jacket. The Cheyenne's head slammed into Jed, ramming him backward. In falling, he kicked his leg up, smashing into the brave's naked belly. The Cheyenne was lifted high, the momentum of his charge carrying him over Jed's head.

Jed leapt onto his feet and spun about, his bowie ready. As the Cheyenne lifted his head dazedly, his own knife gleaming in his right hand, Jed flung himself at him. There was a quick, furious struggle for dominance that ended when Jed pressed his bowie into the Cheyenne's windpipe, then danced clear. As the fountain of blood slowly pulsed to a dribble, Jed wiped off his blade in the grass and sheathed it. He found his rifle and started back toward the stream.

He wasn't pleased with himself. He'd acted too hastily. He could gain no information on the whereabouts of White Cloud's Cheyenne band from a dead brave.

He was near the stream when he saw a flash of white buckskin through trees lining the bank. Someone had reached his dugout and was getting ready to step into it. He moved swiftly, silently closer. Parting a low patch of willows, he stepped clear and found himself looking into the startled face of a Cheyenne woman.

She cringed instinctively, waiting for the tall mountain man to smite her. She was tall, graceful in her bearing, and with a round, pleasing face. Despite her fear, once she realized he wasn't going to strike her down, she regarded him defiantly, her black-cherry eyes smoldering. She wasn't short on courage, and Jed liked that. Meanwhile, she sent daring glances about her, as if she expected her warrior to appear from the brush at any moment to save her from this towering white man.

"He's dead," Jed told her in Comanche.

He pointed back the way he had come and made the sign for death that all plains tribes knew. The sound of the Comanche tongue coming from Jed startled her momentarily, but she understood the situation at once.

Jed found two ponies nearby, along with the

dead warrior's gear packed onto a travois. Proud, yet submissive, the warrior's woman followed along the stream leading the ponies as Jed had indicated, while Jed paddled the dugout back upstream. When he came to a thick growth of riverbank willows, he jumped into the hip-deep water and pushed the dugout toward them. Jed and Tom Fitz had hollowed the dugout by hand from a cottonwood log. It was about eight feet long and disappeared completely into the thick tangle of willows.

Carrying the remaining traps and his rifle, he strode ashore and mounted one of the ponies, indicating to the Cheyenne woman that she should ride the pony pulling the travois. She slid eagerly up onto the pony's back and rode the rest of the way a short distance behind him.

It was clear she was resigned to the fact that she had just exchanged an Indian master for a white one. Indian women knew that white men were notoriously soft where women were concerned. Jed had often heard the Comanche women talking about it. It was said white men seldom beat their women or let them go without food. At times white men even helped their women in their tasks. For men so weak as to allow this, the Comanche women expressed open contempt; yet, whenever they were taken or purchased by a white man, Jed had noticed, they soon forgave their new master his weakness.

"What you got there, hoss?"

It was late and Tom Fitz had a good fire going.

Dropping the firewood he'd been carrying, he walked toward Jed, his eyes taking in eagerly the ponies and the Indian woman.

"Can't you tell?"

"She's a Cheyenne, sure enough. And them is good buffalo ponies, by the looks of them." He grinned at Jed. "I'll bet you found her the same place you found the ponies."

Jed told Tom Fitz the story. At once he made plans to butcher the bear and lug its remains into camp. Bear meat was tough, and it had to be cooked all the way through or it would give you worms. But when the proper precautions were taken, bear meat was as edible as elk or deer.

"With this here black-eyed helper you just brought in to camp, we'll have jerky in no time," he said. "Who gets to sleep with her?"

"You can have her, Tom. She doesn't have all that much appeal to me."

"You gettin' fuzzy in your old age?"

"It isn't that."

"What's her name?"

"Ask her. I don't speak Cheyenne—and while you're at it, find out if she's a Mountain Cheyenne."

"Damn good idea," Tom Fitz said as he and Jed walked over to her.

She watched both men approaching, a wary look in her fathomless eyes. But she didn't turn or run. Come what may, she'd survive. Jed saw this strength in her and felt a sudden admiration for her.

"What's yer name?" Tom Fitz demanded.

She replied in Cheyenne, but neither man could make much of it, nor could they tell if she was telling them her name or complaining about the death of her brave.

Tom Fitz turned to Jed. "Where'd you find her?"

"Near the willows where I was hiding the dugout."

Tom Fitz turned back to the Cheyenne woman. "You, Willow Woman!"

She frowned.

Tom Fitz pointed at her. "You, Willow Woman!"

The woman understood instantly. She struck her chest with her right palm. "Me, Willow Woman."

Tom Fitz glanced at Jed, pleased. "She ain't no complete stranger to English, looks like." Then he pointed to himself, "Me, Tom Fitz."

She nodded quickly. "Tom Fitz," she repeated.

Jed stepped closer and indicated himself. "I am Jed," he told her.

She looked at Jed with her bright button eyes and shook her head solemnly. "No," she said, "you Golden Hawk!"

Using an adroit mixture of sign language and pidgin English, Willow Woman explained she was a member of the Mountain Cheyenne band headed by the war chief White Cloud. Her buck had incurred the wrath of White Cloud when he tried to take the golden-haired woman while she slept. The brave was caught when the white woman drove him off with a knife. The brave's punishment was banishment from the band. Willow

Woman was his wife and had to endure his exile with him.

When Jed asked her why she had addressed him as Golden Hawk, she simply shrugged and repeated her original assertion. He was Golden Hawk.

Tom Fitz looked across the fire at Jed. "Looks like them two Comanches I saw in Concho know where Annabelle is and are waiting for you to come after her."

"Using her for bait."

"And the Mountain Cheyenne know all about it."

Jed looked back at Willow Woman. She'd been listening intently, and he could tell she understood most of what Tom Fitz had said. He leaned close to her.

"Is that right, Willow Woman? Are the Comanches waiting up here for me to come after my sister."

Her face became impassive. He might as well have been talking to a stone. He tried a new tack. "Does Willow Woman want to go home to her people?"

At once she brightened. "Go home to people. Yes."

"Will you take us?"

She hesitated only briefly, then nodded.

Tom Fitz asked Willow Woman how far the tribe was from where they were. It took a while for her to convey the distance to him, but when she had, Tom Fitz looked with some exasperation at Jed.

"No wonder we couldn't find her people. They've drifted north into Snake River country."

"How soon can we pull out?"

"Won't take more'n a few days to check my traps and clear out."

"Good," Jed said.

He looked with sudden affection at Willow Woman. This tall, button-eyed Cheyenne was going to take him to Annabelle. After all this time he'd see his sister again—and keep the promise he made to take her back to her own people at last.

A week later, they reached the mountains that presented the last barrier to the Snake River country. Higher and higher they went, sometimes moving across upland parks, the grass lush, the alders and beach gold now in their autumn splendor. At other times they found themselves clinging to narrow game trails coiled above distant gorges. At such times, Willow Woman led the way. This was her land, and she brightened noticeably with each mile that brought her closer to her people.

She rode her pony while Jed rode the other one. It was a paint, an agile, surefooted animal that never seemed to tire. Tom Fitz rode one of his mules.

On the third night, deep into the mountains, the only place they could find free of mosquitoes that had enough forage for their animals was atop a narrow ridge that connected two steep mountain flanks. The drop from the ridge was almost straight down—on both sides. A tributary of the Snake River wound around the ridge far below them, and the sound it made charging through the narrow gorge drifted up to them like the murmur of a distant sea.

Willow Woman provided a fine meal. As she put away the tin plates and cups, Jed watched her with some satisfaction. Indeed, all that day he'd been aware of her dark eyes watching him. Yet each time he met her gaze, she looked quickly away. He'd made no effort to bed her. And Tom Fitz had asked him the night before if he wanted her, since one of them would have to take her sooner or later. As he put it, she was heating up like a wildcat after a long winter.

At the time, Jed had avoided answering. Not because he didn't want her, he realized ruefully, but because he did. He was simply reluctant to admit to himself and Tom Fitz just how much. Now, as he watched her gather pine boughs for her bed, he wanted to call her over to his sugan. Instead, he lay back and stared up at the bright, starlit sky.

And fell almost immediately asleep.

He came awake suddenly, fighting off the drowsiness that still fogged him. Willow Woman was in his sugan with him, her hand closing like a vise around his solid erection. He'd been dreaming, and the dream had been getting out of hand. Now he knew why. He turned his head to face her, and she fastened her lips hungrily to his.

Insatiable, she fell upon him, her tongue probing wantonly, her warm eager body pressing urgently against his. He felt her moist pubis accepting his erection, then slipped deeper into her hot, moist warmth. With a sigh he rolled over onto her, cleaving her effortlessly. As her tight cleft closed hungrily about his thrusting erection, he flung off the last tendrils of sleep and came fully awake.

In a moment he was thrusting smoothly, deeply, feeling her clinging to him, accepting each thrust with a slight moan of pleasure. He kept his strokes measured, slow, in a deliberate effort to send her over the top. It worked. He felt her hands clawing at his buttocks while her long-limbed frame rose up hungrily to meet each thrust. Then, withdrawing deliberately, he pulled out of her far enough to rest the tip of his erection just inside her labia. She began to moan in frustration, then cried out something in her Cheyenne tongue he didn't understand. It sounded like a curse. Angrily she thrust herself recklessly up at him, her muff devouring his waiting erection.

With a laugh, he plunged recklessly down into her, impaling her on his fiery lance. The shock of it caused her to shudder with delight. She flung her arms around his neck. No more games now. Wildly aroused, he caught her mouth with his, entwined his tongue about hers, and began humping her like a crazed billy goat. Her arms still wrapped about his neck, she clung to him, groaning in ecstasy. Her climax came suddenly, with a rush. Shuddering wildly, she flung herself upward, arching her back. Hung there, clinging to him, frozen in space, she climaxed, a moaning cry bursting from her lips. It sounded like the night cry of a she-cougar.

Jed slammed down onto her, driving home with an urgency as powerful as hers—and the dam broke. In a series of powerful ejaculations, he came and came again, emptying his seed deep within her.

Rolling off her, he drifted into a drugged, totally satiated sleep. The last thing he remembered was her cool hands stroking his face, her soft lips laving his face, her voice lulling him.

It was still night when Willow Woman awoke him the second time. He was on his back and her upper torso was over his face as she braced herself on her two arms. She was planted firmly down onto his sleeping erection and was rocking slowly back and forth, her breasts swaying gently, a nipple occasionally brushing his face.

She had already, magically, brought him close to another climax. When she saw him looking up at her, she smiled, lowered her lips to his, and kissed him, her tongue probing lightly at his lips, laving them with fire. He began rocking back and forth urgently. Laughing softly, she released his lips and sat back so she could work herself down still farther onto his erection.

Faster and faster she drove down upon him, her dark hair billowing as she flung her head from side to side. Abruptly, she flung her head back, then came in an explosive, shuddering spasm. The muscles inside her squeezed him so tightly, he thought he was going to break off inside her.

And then, in an explosive rush, he came, firing repeatedly up into her, bucking wildly with each spasm. Hanging on to him, she shrieked softly, coming with him, again and again, until she collapsed forward onto him, her cheek resting on his powerful chest. Lying back quietly, her warmth covering him, Jed stroked her hair as his spent organ receded gently from her moistness.

"Mmm," she murmured softly, rolling off him.

A moment later, as he fell into a delicious, drugged sleep, the last thing he felt was her soft lips placing a kiss on his brow.

Willow Woman was bent over him, shaking him awake for the third time that night. He blinked up at her. He couldn't believe she needed more. Naked, her dark hair falling over him like a tent, she kept shaking him.

"Go back to sleep," he told her, angry for the first time.

"Comanches," she hissed.

Jed was awake in an instant and spotted Lame Deer moving quickly toward them. He flung Willow Woman to one side, reached behind his neck for his throwing knife, and sent it at the onrushing Comanche. The blade sank deep into Lame Deer's chest, but the Comanche yanked the knife out of his chest and kept coming. Jed rolled aside, and kept rolling. Lame Deer changed direction, but the deep knife wound was beginning to take its toll. He stumbled, then recovered enough to fling his hatchet. It nicked Jed's skull, momentarily stunning him.

Lame Deer flung himself onto Jed, his hunting knife gleaming in the moonlight. In one savage, deadly stroke, he brought it down. The blade sliced deep into Jed's left shoulder. Jed pulled the knife out of his shoulder and turned with it to strike Lame Deer. But the Comanche caught Jed's wrist and twisted it. Jed dropped the knife. As Lame Deer grabbed for it, Willow Woman rushed out of the night and kicked it into the brush.

While Lame Deer was momentarily distracted by Willow Woman, Jed smashed through him, flung himself back to his sugan, and snatched up his Walker Colt. Spinning around, he cocked the weapon and fired at the Comanche. The round took off Lame Deer's right ear, but it still didn't stop him. Jed cocked again, but before he could fire, Lame Deer kicked the revolver out of his hand and leapt upon him.

Weaponless, both men grappled clumsily on the ground. The warm blood pouring from both their wounds made each one difficult for the other to hold. Snatching up a stone, Lame Deer smashed it into Jed's chin, knocking him onto his back.

As Jed lay back, his senses reeling from the blow, Lame Deer jumped up and began kicking him about the head and face, attempting to crush his windpipe. Through a red haze Jed saw the Comanche's foot slamming down on him over and over, saw the ugly black strokes of war paint on Lame Deer's face. In that instant he recalled another cruel hand-to-hand struggle a long ten years before. And remembered too his mother's screams.

He felt anger then. Anger powerful enough to send a surging, colossal strength through every muscle in his body. Transformed, he reached up and grabbed Lame Deer's ankle with both hands, then twisted. Lame Deer cried out and spun around as Jed rose to his feet and continued to twist the Comanche's ankle. Lame Deer flopped onto his back, beating the ground in agony. Jed dragged him to the edge of the clearing and with one final burst of energy flung him far out into the gorge.

"Watch out, Jed," Tom Fitz cried.

Jed spun around. Tom Fitz was on the ground, his face covered with blood. And racing toward Jed, his long buffalo knife held high, was Hungry Horse.

Jed waited calmly. A second before Hungry Horse struck him, he went down on all fours, then drove forward with his right shoulder, slamming into the Comanche just above his knees. Hungry Horse went flying over Jed, his momentum carrying him to the edge of the ridge. Loose stones and gravel shot out from under his moccasined feet. He dropped his knife and scrambled for a handhold, then went over, disappearing without a cry.

Jed peered over the edge. Less than five feet below him, Hungry Horse's painted face stared up at him. The Comanche was clinging with both hands to a rock jutting out of the canyon wall. For only a moment did Jed hesitate. Then, blood still welling from his knife wound, he lay flat and reached down to grab Hungry Horse by the wrist and haul him to safety.

Before he could do so, Hungry Horse's face twisted into a snarl. He spat up at Jed, then let go. Twisting slowly, he vanished into the black void. The Comanche would die rather than accept the gift of life from Golden Hawk.

Jed didn't attempt to sleep any more than night.

—9—

A week later Willow Woman was babbling about a big snow when they crossed a pine-studded ridge and descended into a lush valley. Here, she indicated, her people would be settling into their winter quarters. Clumps of alders and birch spotted the landscape, and as they rode, Jed couldn't help glorying in the clear air and in the sight of the distant, snow-capped mountains that ringed the land. The caps of snow sat high in the sky like massive, benign gods.

Jed and Tom Fitz had fully recovered from their wounds, and both regarded Willow Woman with much affection. Had she not warned Jed, then later kicked that weapon away from Lame Deer, both men would probably be rotting at the foot of that gorge.

Astride their mounts, they wound down through the patches of timber, breaking out occasionally onto the parklike stretches of meadowland. They spotted elk, mule deer, and on the ridges an occasional coyote. The land was rich. If winter was near, it was difficult to imagine it, so pleasantly warm was it.

When they hit a long flat stretch, then rode through a wet, swampy area, they noted how excited Willow Woman was getting. Jed could tell she was eager to ride ahead to greet her people. He glanced at Tom Fitz. Tom nodded and grinned. Turning to Willow Woman, Jed motioned her on ahead of them. Flashing him a pleased smile, she flicked her pony with the ends of her reins and swept on ahead, the travois bumping ludicrously after her.

About half an hour later, they saw the smoke from the Cheyenne encampment's tepees coming from beyond the next ridge.

"Looks like quite a few lodges," Tom Fitz remarked, moving up alongside Jed.

"I don't like it," Jed told him, frowning.

"What's wrong?"

"The smoke. It doesn't look like it's coming from campfires."

"Jesus!"

Jed spurred his pony ahead, Tom Fitz urging his mule on after him.

They found the encampment in ruins. Fires were coming from lodges that had been pulled down onto their hearth fires. A few Cheyenne women, wailing and tearing at themselves, were stumbling about among the dead. Everywhere Jed looked he saw the sprawled, lifeless bodies of men, women, and children. Wounded braves, arrows protruding from their slumped torsos, lay in their own blood. From out of the brush surrounding the encampment, a few Cheyenne men and women emerged, staring about them in shocked dismay.

Galloping into the encampment, looking about wildly for Annabelle, Jed caught sight of Willow Woman draped over the bodies of an old man and woman. She lay frighteningly still. He leapt from his pony and knelt by her side.

"Willow Woman!"

She didn't respond. He turned her over. In her grief she had mutilated herself terribly. She had lopped off all the fingers of her left hand, and that not being enough, she had slashed wildly at her breasts, using her blade too recklessly. She had slashed an artery. Staring up at him in death, her black-cherry eyes held no luster. Jed closed them gently, then stood up and craned his head anxiously as he looked about.

What of Annabelle? If this was White Cloud's band, had she escaped during the attack—or was she already dead, sprawled among these broken, mutilated bodies?

Tom Fitz rode up.

"Find Annabelle!" Jed told him.

But by nightfall, they had found no sign of her. It was a Blackfoot war party that had attacked the village, they learned, and Annabelle had been carried off. The few survivors wanted nothing to do with Jed or Tom Fitz as they went about burying their dead and moaning out their grief. Their band was finished, and they knew it. Now they would be Cheyenne without a history as their few surviving members became part of larger Cheyenne bands on the plains below.

At last Tom Fitz found an old, wrinkled camp chief willing to talk to them, a survivor who had managed to kill two of the attacking Blackfeet. They had seen the old man stoically pull from his side a Blackfoot arrow and then wrap the wound tightly with strips of buckskin.

Now, crouched on a small knoll above his destroyed village, Tom Fitz gave the Indian tobacco for his pipe. After he had lit his pipe and passed it around, the camp chief told them of the attack. It had come at dawn, with a ferocity that was the hallmark of the Blackfoot. As far south as the Staked Plains, Jed had heard of these fierce and terrible Blackfoot warriors from whom no other plains tribe were safe. They usually struck at dawn and with a silent, deadly thoroughness that decimated entire villages—just as they had done here.

The old chief told them that White Cloud had been struck down in the first assault while his women, all of whom had remained at his side, fought as ferociously as any brave. The golden-haired one had fought well also, but she had been struck down by a war hatchet, then carried off. Since her beauty and courage were known throughout the mountains, her capture was a great coup for the Blackfeet. Puffing reflectively on his pipe, the old chief believed that if she lived she'd be taken as a wife by the great chief of the Blackfeet, Tall Buffalo. And this, to the old chief, seemed altogether fitting and proper.

There was nothing more the old camp chief could tell Jed and Tom Fitz. Tom Fitz thanked him, gave him a pouch filled generously with tobacco, and watched him walk slowly back to the still-smoldering village, the tail of his blanket dragging forlornly on the ground behind him.

The two men walked back to their waiting animals. Jed mounted his pony, Tom Fitz his mule. For a moment, they looked back at the village. Even from this distance they could still hear the women and old people wailing.

"I'm going after the Blackfeet," Jed told Tom Fitz.

"Then you ain't goin' alone."

"Yes I am."

"Dammit! You'll get eaten alive by them Blackfeet!"

"I don't think so."

Tom Fitz looked at Jed. Then he shrugged. "I guess maybe not. Maybe you'll eat them up. One by one. If'n you come out of this, hoss, you know where to find me."

"Thanks, Tom."

Tom Fitz stuffed some tobacco leaves into his cheek, turned his mule, and started back up the slope.

There was no need for him to say anything more to Jed—not because he didn't feel sorrow at this parting but because Tom Fitz knew there were never any words for what a man truly felt.

Reading sign the Blackfeet in their arrogance made no effort to cover, Jed saw that they had split into two war parties ten miles farther into the mountains. It took him a while to ascertain which of the parties had taken Annabelle. He followed the largest war party for two miles at least until he found no sign of Annabelle's presence, then doubled back and took after the other, smaller war party. Before a mile had passed, he caught sight of a few strands of blond hair clinging to a berry bush.

He felt immediate elation. The Blackfeet in this war party would be easier to take one by one.

When he saw the hoofprint in the soft ground ahead of him, he slipped from the pony and went down on one knee to examine it. The imprint was clean, which meant it had been made after daylight—a track left at night would have revealed tiny insect tracks. He mounted up and kept going, more warily now, his senses alert for more sign.

Then he saw the eagle. It was beginning to circle in the sky ahead of him. After two turns it flapped away to the west. Jed halted the pony and stayed for a long while in the shadow of a pine, listening. Then he dismounted. When an eagle found itself above a man, it circled or flew the other way. Apparently the Blackfoot party he was tracking was not far ahead of him and was still moving east.

After checking to make sure it would have plenty of forage, Jed tethered his pony to a sapling and slipped into the woods. He left his rifle behind, carrying with him only his bowie and throwing knife and the Walker Colt, a weapon he hoped he wouldn't have to use. He had gone not more than a hundred yards when he froze and moved swiftly against a tree.

For five minutes at least he stood against the tree, waiting. The timber was silent—too silent. The birds had flown; the squirrels and other small game had fled to their burrows. Man, the great destroyer, was about.

Jed waited.

The sound of a moccasined foot crushing a pine bough came from Jed's right. Immediately he ducked low and turned. An arrow slammed into the tree inches above his head and out of a nearby clump of alders a Blackfoot rushed at him, his war club raised over his head. Jed flung up his bowie, holding it like a sword, then lunged forward before the Blackfoot could bring down his war club. The Indian took the entire blade in his gut. Jed sliced upward until the blade struck his brisket, then flung the Blackfoot over his shoulder. Crouching, he waited for more Blackfeet.

But none came. That single Blackfoot had been sent back to check the rear. Soon, others would follow to find out what had happened to him. But meanwhile, Jed had some time. He turned around. The Blackfoot was slumped loosely at the foot of the tree. Jed circled his scalp with the top of his bowie, then snapped off the Blackfoot's scalp. He hung it on his belt, hefted the dead Indian onto his shoulder, and clambered up into the tree. When he judged himself to be high enough, he wedged the body in among some branches, then climbed swiftly down. Cutting off a branch, he brushed away any sign of struggle, after which he moved on through the timber.

He heard the Blackfeet warriors before he saw them. Moving with absolute silence through the timber, he parted a thicket and peered at the Blackfeet war party. They had set up a noonday camp beside a stream. There were seven Blackfeet in Jed's line of sight.

He didn't see Annabelle.

Moving to a different vantage point, he caught sight of her off to his left, sitting down, her back against a tree. She had wrapped herself in a torn blanket and there was a bloody bandage around the upper portion of her left arm. When Jed looked at her closely, he was startled. Her long blond hair had been cut short and was dark with grease. The cast of her face was sullen, even despairing. She looked older than her years.

A Blackfoot warrior with the arrogant bearing of a war chief stepped out of a patch of brush beside Annabelle and stood looking down at her. His hair was rolled into a hornlike topknot and was wrapped with red felt strips. He said a few words to Annabelle that sounded like a command from where Jed crouched, but she didn't respond, her blue eyes remaining icily contemptuous as she stared defiantly across the stream. The Blackfoot struck the back of her head with his quirt, driving her forward. Without looking at him or uttering a sound, Annabelle sat back up and continued to stare across the stream.

The Blackfoot stalked off.

Jed waited. He had to be sure that these eight were all the Blackfeet he had to contend with. At last, he slipped back into the timber and circled the encampment until he found their ponies farther down the stream. A single young Blackfoot warrior was guarding them.

With infinite patience Jed crept up behind the Blackfoot. Not until the Indian felt Jed's forearm closing about his windpipe did he know of Jed's presence. Jed drew him back swiftly, feeling the windpipe crunch. The Blackfoot slumped, lifeless, in his fierce embrace. Again Jed took a scalp and climbed a tree, wedging his second dead Blackfoot between branches well hidden from the ground below. On the ground he slashed through the rawhide line holding the ponies and drove them silently downstream. He kept them going for a mile at least, then turned back to the Blackfoot encampment.

Within a few hundred yards of it, Jed heard two warriors moving noisily through the brush toward him as they followed the tracks left by their ponies. He slipped to one side and waited for them. Brushing impatiently through the brush, they trotted swiftly along, obviously eager to overtake the ponies.

One of them hung back nervously, looking about him warily as he trotted after his companion. Jed slipped out of the brush at his side and clamped one hand over his mouth as he drove his bowie into the Blackfoot's liver. Gasping, the fellow crumpled. His companion turned. Jed reached back and sent his throwing knife at him. The blade buried itself in his chest directly over the heart. The Indian stopped and tugged at the knife, pulling it out finally. He dropped the knife and took a step toward Jed, then toppled facedown onto the forest floor.

Again Jed busied himself taking scalps and disposing of the bodies.

It was dusk when Jed moved to within a few yards of the remaining six Blackfeet. Despite the sudden chill that had fallen over the timber, they sat huddled without a fire. They were frightened. Their medicine had lost its power. Their ponies had disappeared along with four members of their war party.

The war chief had a brief parley with his braves. At its conclusion, two Blackfeet took up their weapons and moved out, evidently in search of their four missing warriors. Jed moved out also, cutting a trail that would bring him around in front of the closest Blackfoot. Then he climbed a pine tree, crouched on the lowest branch, and waited. When at last he saw the shadowy form moving in his direction, he shook the branch slightly. A pinecone dropped to the forest floor.

The Blackfoot caught the sound and headed directly for the tree, peering cautiously about him on all sides as he approached. Not once, however, did he look up. As he passed under Jed, Jed dropped, his bowie slashing down, slicing neatly through the Blackfoot's jugular.

As the warrior dropped, Jed heard running feet. He turned as the second Blackfoot brave was rushing at him. Jed sheathed his bowie, reached up for a branch, and lifted himself. In one swift move, he swung though the air toward the onrushing warrior, his feet slamming into the Blackfoot's chest. The brave went down under Jed's onslaught, crunching backward into a bed of pine brush. Dazed, the Blackfoot stared up at Jed, then opened his mouth to cry out. But Jed's powerful fingers closed about his throat, then shook him violently until his neck snapped.

Jed scalped the two dead warriors, then carried each of them into a separate tree and wedged them into the branches as he had the others. Remaining high in the tree, he cupped his hands about his mouth and made the call of the Cannibal Owl. Once, twice, three times, he uttered the stuttering shriek, then dropped to the forest floor and slipped swiftly back toward the stream and the Blackfoot encampment.

Within sight of it, he lay flat, inching close under a downed log and watched. He could see the suppressed terror on the faces of the four remaining Blackfeet. They had heard the cry of the Cannibal Owl—and they knew what that meant.

The war chief sent a brave out to search for their vanished comrades. He came back alone. Another was sent out. And another. Each one came back alone, shivering with terror. Dawn came at last with no sign of their fellow warriors. The ground had swallowed them up. Or the Cannibal Owl, the Comanche demon who descended in the dark to devour men and whose monstrous bones still dotted the plains.

Night fell. It was too cold to endure without a fire, so a huge bonfire was built to warm not only their bodies but their chilled souls. Jed waited until midnight, then ran out over the small clearing. The glare of the fire made it impossible for those on the ground to see through it to Jed crouched on the branch.

Annabelle, still wrapped in her blanket, remained close by the stream, watching the four Blackfeet warily. She seemed alert now, aware, as were the Blackfeet, that something awful was afoot, something for which there was no explanation or defense. Her alertness told Jed that she knew, as did he, that in this state, the Blackfeet were capable of anything. Indeed, if things got any worse, there was always the chance they would slit her throat out of sheer terror.

It was time now for Jed to make his move. Uttering the cry of the Cannibal Owl, he flung the scalps of the six dead warriors onto the stream bank. With a shriek, the Blackfeet jumped up, cowering, their eyes on the bloody trophies. Jed dropped lightly to the ground behind them and flung his throwing knife at the closest Blackfoot. The blade sank deep into his back, just above his kidney. The other three whirled around to face him. Jed fired his Colt at the war chief. The round caught him in the face and he staggered back, then sank to one knee.

Jed's sudden appearance was too much for the remaining two warriors. They had concluded that their medicine had lost all its power, and caught in the terrible fire of Jed's overwhelming medicine, they could think of only one thing: to flee. They leapt off the embankment into the stream. One, a poor swimmer obviously, was immediately caught up in the swift water and pulled under. The other Blackfoot managed to scramble ashore on the far side and vanish into the timber.

"Jed," cried Annabelle, rushing into his arms.

Jed caught his sister in his arms and held her close, unable for a moment to believe that he had done it, that he had kept his promise to her.

"I thought you'd never find me," Annabelle cried.

She buried her face in his broad chest and began to sob as if her heart would break. Jed kept his arms about her, murmuring soft, reassuring words of comfort. It was strange. He had found Annabelle at last and taken her from her captors just as he had promised her he would. But there was not the triumph or the feeling of exultation he had expected.

He held her still closer, wishing there were some way he could wipe out the years between Kentucky and this moment, some magic potion that would make Annabelle forget all the shame and cruelty she had endured. But there was no such potion.

She wouldn't be comforted, it seemed. Too much, he realized, had happened to her. Far too much.

—10—

The next day Jed went downstream after the Blackfeet's ponies and selected one for himself and one for Annabelle. They started south, heading for Bent's Fort. The first snow began to fall two days later, while they were still in high country, and at once Jed remembered Willow Woman telling them about the big snow that she had been certain was coming.

When the wind picked up and they could no longer buck the driving snow, Jed made a camp of sorts in among some rocks, then constructed a roof of branches and pine boughs. For three days and two nights, they huddled over a pathetic fire, shivering under the two blankets they had with them, eating little, subsisting almost entirely on coffee. By the time the storm had blown itself out, the world had been transformed. Shoulder-high drifts were everywhere.

It took Jed two days to bring down any fresh

game—two rabbits and a partridge. Annabelle did what she could with such meager fare and then they set off through the blinding glare. They struggled across a gleaming white wilderness of snow and ice, becoming weaker with each passing day, breaking ground for their ponies most of the time.

Annabelle looked worse each day. She hadn't been well when she had been taken by the Blackfeet, she confessed to Jed. Their treatment of her hadn't helped any. It was her lungs she complained of the most. She couldn't seem to get enough air into them. At night, wrapped in her sugan, she coughed raggedly in her sleep, and before long Jed noticed the hectic flush in her cheeks.

She had a fever.

The bitter irony of all this wasn't lost on Jed. He had rescued his sister from her captors. It was all either of them had wanted for the past ten years—to be free. Yet, if Jed didn't provide adequate shelter and bring down fresh meat for his sister soon, he'd lose her to a remorseless and far more final captor.

They pushed on through a pass and found the snow on the other side much less deep. Pressing on, they came to a valley and saw patches of grass and boulders thrusting up through the snow cover. In another day they found the wind much less punishing, the snow not much deeper than their ponies' fetlocks. They had outdistanced winter. On the third day beyond the pass, they sighted a cabin perched on a high ridge and immediately headed for it.

Behind the cabin was the privy and alongside that a barn big enough to shelter their ponies. There was even a corral back of the barn. As they rode into the yard, Jed caught sight of a rusted heap of traps in one corner of the corral. And looking still closer, he saw the bleached skeleton propped up against a corral post, a rusted rifle still clutched in his hand.

Annabelle saw it at about the same time he did. She groaned softly and looked away, but said nothing.

"I'll take care of that," he told her as he dismounted, then helped her down off her pony.

She smiled wanly at him. "He's not doing any harm there. Maybe his ghost will protect us."

"I'll bury him out back. His bones need a rest."

"I wonder who he was."

"Maybe we'll find out inside."

They went into the cabin. From the looks of it, the place must have been abandoned for more than a year. The leather hinges on the door had almost rotted away and there was not a trace of the oiled paper that had been used in the windows. The pounded-dirt floor was spotted by weeds that had burst through it. A leak in the roof had scoured out a channel all the way across the floor and out under the door frame. The window frames needed repairing and the logs chinked with fresh mud.

Jed left Annabelle inside and explored the slope behind the cabin. Following a well-worn path, he came upon a mountain spring. At the rate it was flowing, he judged there would be plenty of water through the winter, if it came to that.

He returned to the cabin. Annabelle was resting in a rickety chair by the deal table, her face wan, her eyes bright with fever. She attempted a smile as he stepped inside.

"Feels good to sit on a chair," she told him.

"We'll stay here for a while," he said. "There's a spring back there. I can fix the leak in the roof and I can cover the windows, too. Once I clean out that chimney and the fireplace, we'll have a fire going."

Annabelle nodded and got to her feet. "I'll get some firewood."

"You stay right there. Rest up. This is going to be Home Sweet Home for a while."

She didn't protest and Jed went out to find a shovel so he could bury the mountain man who had died defending the place.

For the next couple of weeks, Jed's Hawken spoke out and soon their table groaned with fresh meat and all the roots and tubers he could dig out of the riverbank a few miles below the cabin. There were potatoes and flour and small sacks of beans in among the provisions Tom Fitz had given him before they parted. Soon, Annabelle's lungs cleared and she began to sleep for long blessed stretches. Her eyes grew bright with health, not fever, and she began to take an active, eager interest in the world about them. A warm spell had them out hunting together, and for Jed this valley became a paradise.

Come spring, he promised Annabelle, they would make it all the way to Bent's Fort, and from there, Independence would be only a short jump. They would both be back in Kentucky by midsummer to astonish their relatives at their miraculous survival.

"What's wrong?" he asked, sitting up.

From across the room, he heard Annabelle stirring. "What do you mean? You hear something?"

"That's just it. I don't hear anything. Anything at all."

He got up and went to the door. There was no sense in trying to look out the windows. He had chinked them up crudely to keep out the wind. He pushed the door open and felt something on the other side pushing just as strongly against him. But he managed to open it a crack and look out. He had gone to sleep with the memory of a bright moon gleaming like a silver coin in the night sky.

There was no longer any moon and the feel of snow on his face told him what was happening. A steady, constant snowfall was sifting down out of the sky, covering the world around them in a vast blanket of silence. He stuck his head out farther and listened. He could hear the snow falling, a quiet, comforting sound.

He pulled the door shut behind him and glanced over at Annabelle. "It's come," he said. "Winter."

"We'll be safe now."

"Safe?"

"From the Blackfeet, from Tall Buffalo."

Until that moment he hadn't realized that Annabelle had been living in constant fear that the Blackfeet would make another attempt to capture her. He smiled in the darkness at her. "He and his people are busy bedding down for the winter. They don't have any time to come after you."

Annabelle didn't reply as she lay back down and pulled her blankets up over her shoulder.

Jed stood for a moment in the darkness, listening at the door, then moved back to his cot.

A lone gray wolf had been prowling along the ridge above the cabin for the past week. At night its haunting wail had brought them both upright in their cots. On the first really clear night, Jed decided it was time for him to go out and bring him down.

"Do you have to?" Annabelle asked.

"He's keeping us both awake. I've seen his tracks. He's big enough for you to make me a fine hooded winter coat out of the fur."

"All right. How long will you be gone?"

"I don't know."

She nodded and looked back at the fire. She was wearing his clothes now, his extra pair of leggings and his buckskin shirt, which she had altered with bone needles and the sinews of the small game Jed had shot for their table. He had watched her drying and preparing the sinews and sewing in the light of the fire—working as diligently and as silently as any Indian. Every once in a while, if she pricked her finger or made a mistake, she would swear softly in Cheyenne.

But never in Comanche.

He waited in the tree. It gave him a clear, unobstructed view of the ridge. The wolf had howled for a full minute or so when he first came out. But in the past hour there had been no sound from him. An incredible, pristine silence had fallen over the world. For weeks the snow had been piling up, and though he had fashioned crude snowshoes for himself, it had still been difficult to make his way up the steep slope to this ridge. Pulling himself into the tree while carrying the Hawken hadn't been easy, either. The loaded branches had sifted snow down upon him constantly, at times covering him from head to foot.

The wolf called again.

This time his howl came from just beyond the ridge. Jed turned carefully in the tree and lifted the Hawken, waiting. He was in luck. The steady wind was in his face, carrying his scent away from the wolf. The wolf, spilling the snow ahead of him as he loped along, appeared on the crest of the ridge, standing out clearly in the bright moonlight. He was coming directly toward Jed. Jed rested his cheek on the Hawken's stock and coiled his finger lightly about the trigger.

The wolf kept coming on. He was a big one, all right. A hooded coat made from such a wolf would be a fine one indeed. When the wolf was within fifty yards, Jed caressed the trigger. The recoil was slight. The crack of the detonation echoed sharply throughout the valley. The wolf leapt in the air, then flopped over into the snow. Jed waited to see if he still had life in him. But Jed must have hit what he had aimed at, the powerful chest and the heart that beat within, for the wolf didn't move again.

He pushed open the door, strode in, and flung the big wolf down on the floor in front of the fire.

"Tomorrow we'll skin it," he told Annabelle.

Relief had flooded her face at his appearance. She managed a smile. "It will make a fine coat."

He leaned his rifle against the fireplace and closed his arms around her. Her heart was still beating wildly, fearfully, like a frantic bird trying to escape capture. She must have been terrified waiting alone in the cabin for him to return— and what terrors that single rifle shot must have aroused in her, even though her common sense should have told her it was him firing on the wolf.

Not until she was well out of this country would she be able to live without the constant fear of recapture.

In the days that followed, Jed watched his sister scrape the wolf's skin clean, stretch it, cut it, then begin the laborious task of sewing through the pelt. She worked with a steady, patient tenacity that seemed to ease her mind. At times he heard her humming snatches of tunes he had never heard before. Cheyenne songs, he had no doubt.

Smoking a crude pipe he had fashioned for himself, he watched her, contented. Her hair was clean once more and growing. It reached now clear to her shoulders. Color had returned to her cheeks and her face glowed with vitality.

Every now and then she would need him for fitting and he would stand patiently as her deft fingers folded and fastened the heavy fur with her sharp bone needles. It was to be a hip-long coat, and already Jed was imagining himself striding through the snow with it on. Later, he told himself, if he came upon another wolf, he would bring it down also, so Annabelle could make herself just as fine a winter coat.

Annabelle was shaking him awake.

"What is it?" he asked, reaching for the Colt he kept under his pillow.

"Come to the door and see."

He wrapped his blanket around him and padded on bare feet to the door. She pushed it open wider for him and pointed. Below them, following the contour of the valley, a herd of elk was moving to their lower winter pastures. He'd been complaining of the lack of big game for the past few days.

He grinned, dressed quickly, shrugged into his wolfskin jacket, and hurried out of the cabin. He was downwind of the herd and was able to gain a small patch of pine less than a hundred yards from the elk before he was sighted by the leader.

The snow was deep enough to hamper their progress, however, and Jed picked out a big fat buck and brought him down with a single shot from his Hawken.

As the sound of his rifle's crack reverberated off the snow-clad slopes, he hurried from the pines to see to his kill. From a thick stand of timber to his left, a hawk-faced old warrior nudged his horse into the clearing. At the route he was taking, he would be able to cut Jed off from the fallen elk.

Jed pulled up, simmering, and waited for the old Indian's intentions to be made clear. The Indian turned his horse in the belly-deep snow and headed directly up the slope toward Jed. Before he reached Jed, he extended his arm, palm forward, the traditional greeting that meant he came in peace.

Jed relaxed, puzzled.

The old Indian pulled his blankets up closer around his neck, then halted his pony a few feet from Jed. From the Appaloosa pony he was riding and his tasseled, highly decorated quiver, Jed knew at once that this was an old Nez Percé warrior.

"Greetings to Golden Hawk," the Nez Percé said solemnly and with great respect.

It always amazed Jed how swiftly gossip spread between tribes, even those tribes that weren't friendly. To have been addressed in this fashion by an Indian belonging to a tribe Jed had never before encountered shook Jed. Until that moment he had thought of himself and Annabelle as living in snowbound isolation from the rest of the tribes in the region. Now he realized how foolish had been such an estimate of their situation.

Jed acknowledged the greeting with a slight forward nod of his head. "And who is this wise old war chief that greets Golden Hawk in friendship?"

"Joseph Bear. I am Christian Indian who has come back to his people."

"You speak good English."

"I go to missionary school once."

"How do you know of Golden Hawk?"

"That is what our enemies call you."

"Your enemies?"

"The Blackfeet. They say you came in the night like the Cannibal Owl. You devoured six of their braves and spit out their scalps. And you take back from them your sister, the golden-haired one."

"If the Nez Percé are enemies of the Blackfeet, Golden Hawk is pleased to count the Nez Percé as his friends and allies."

The old man glanced at the fallen elk.

"I have just killed this elk." Jed said. "There is too much for Golden Hawk and his sister. Will my friend Joseph Bear share in my good fortune? It would bring honor to me."

The old man brightened. "My lodge has little meat this winter. My daughter, Sable Hair Woman, is very hungry. And it will make me famous again to say I am Golden Hawk's friend."

A moment later, after decapitating the elk and

dressing it into two halves, they attached one half to a length of rawhide and, using Joseph Bear's pony, dragged it up the slope to the cabin. Then they hauled it up onto a hook hanging over the door of the barn to let the blood drain.

From the cabin door, open just a crack, Annabelle watched Jed and Joseph Bear struggle with the steaming carcass. It was clear she didn't trust the Indian. Realizing this, Jed didn't invite the old chief into the cabin. Joseph Bear didn't seem to mind, however, and with a dignified farewell, he mounted his pony and rode back down the slope to claim his gift.

Jed followed him part of the way down the slope, then held up to watch. The last he saw of Joseph Bear was when he disappeared about fifteen minutes later through a narrow pass on the far side of the valley. It seemed that he and Annabelle had for neighbors a band of Nez Percé Indians settling into their winter encampment.

He walked back up the slope to the cabin to get a longer knife for the butchering. As he stepped into the cabin, he told Annabelle who the Indian was, leaving out how the old chief had greeted him.

Two days later they awoke to find just outside their cabin a delegation of Nez Percé Indians waiting patiently on their ponies. Taking his loaded Hawken with him, Jed stepped out to greet them. Joseph Bear was in the lead and again he raised his hand in friendship.

Jed returned the gesture, but he didn't like this.

"My heart is heavy," said Joseph Bear. "He must bring his friend Golden Hawk bad news."

"Golden Hawk is ready for such news," Jed responded, his hands tightening around the Hawken's breach.

"The Nez Percé do not wish to arouse the anger of the great Golden Hawk. So they warn him. Blackfeet approach. They search for Golden Hawk to erase the shame of their earlier defeat."

"Have the Nez Percé told the Blackfeet where Golden Hawk is?"

All the Indians stirred unhappily at this question. Joseph Bear's old seamed face went gray at such an accusation. "No," he said. "We tell Blackfeet nothing. We do not have council with the Bloods."

"Good. Golden Hawk thanks his friend Joseph Bear and his Nez Percé brothers."

This seemed to please the delegation. Joseph Bear raised his right hand in salute. The delegation parted for him, and he rode to its head, leading the Indians back down the slope.

Jed went back inside and closed the cabin door. Annabelle was standing with her back to the fireplace. She had heard everything from the door and was obviously alarmed.

"We'd better leave this valley," Jed said.

"When?"

"In a few days?"

She nodded. He thought he saw relief on her face, but couldn't tell for sure. At once she turned to the fireplace and began to slice for stripping more of the elk's hide. They would need much more pemmican if they were to travel any distance this far into winter.

It was close to dusk. This would be their last day in the valley. They were moving out the next morning. Jed was tracking an otter; the fresh otter meat would take them a long way.

He was above the cabin, and as he stole into the pines, he glanced down the slope and saw the smoke coiling up from the cabin's chimney. Then he concentrated on the otter, sure he could still see its gleaming hide. He carefully brushed aside a snow-laden branch without dislodging a single flake, moved past it successfully, then moved close to a tree and brought up his rifle. The otter turned and looked directly at him, his bewhiskered face intent.

Then it vanished.

Cursing silently, Jed lowered his rifle, turned, and started from the pines. They'd just have to do without fresh meat. As he stepped out of the pines, he became aware of a preternatural silence and felt the hair stand up on the back of his neck. Something was wrong.

Annabelle's despairing scream cut through the waiting silence.

Jed plunged through the snow to the edge of the slope and looked down. Four Blackfeet were dragging Annabelle from the cabin. They were on foot and must have picketed their ponies in the pines at the bottom of the slope. Jed brought up his Hawken, aimed at the closest Blackfoot, and squeezed off a shot. The Blackfoot fell to the ground. Jed rammed home a second charge, aimed again, and fired. A second Blackfoot stumbled, tried to keep going, then spilled forward into the snow.

The remaining two Blackfeet were in the middle of the slope well out in front of the cabin with no cover for hundreds of yards on either side of them. As Jed reloaded, he saw Annabelle break free of the Blackfoot holding her. Jed smiled grimly. This gave him two clear shots.

A forearm swept down over his face, slamming back against his throat. He dropped his rifle and flung himself backward. As he did so, he felt the sharp, needlelike point of a knife driving into his back, just under his ribs. He felt the shock of it clear to his back teeth. Nevertheless, he rolled over onto his attacker, unsheathing his bowie.

He found himself grappling with Little Fox.

"Little Fox!" Jed cried. "You?"

"Yes, Golden Hawk," he spat.

Jed's momentary astonishment gave way to rage. Ignoring the searing pain in his back, he pulled back and hauled Little Fox upright, then thrust his bowie deep into his stomach. Little Fox grunted in pain, then smiled at the man who had once saved his life. As he fell back, he sliced upward with both hands and Jed felt Little Fox's lance slice up into his chest.

Jed tumbled backward into the snow. He managed to pull the lance free, then began to roll over and over down the slope, dimly aware of the blade hilt protruding from his back, digging in deeper with each turn. He kept on slamming through brush and past boulders until the bright, spinning world dimmed into darkness.

And the sound of Annabelle's screams had faded completely.

The wind was howling when Jed opened his eyes and saw a dark-eyed woman bending over him. She had long hair tied back with strips of green felt. Behind her Jed saw Joseph Bear and the snout of an Appaloosa. He heard someone call her Sable Hair Woman. She stepped back to let strong hands lift him out of a closed space and up into a howling blizzard. He was icy cold clear to the marrow of his bones. Any movement he made was painful. He tried to cry out, but nothing came and he passed out.

When next he awoke, he was being lifted off a travois. The wind was shrieking like a chorus of devils as he was carried through it into a lodge so warm he thought he had been deposited into one of hell's ovens. He could hear his voice crying out in rapid Comanche and saw Sable Hair Woman's astonishment at the torrent of abuse that flowed from him.

Then he was being wrapped in furs, and he dropped off into a disordered sleep.

A wooden spoon in one hand, a bowl of broth in the other, Sable Hair Woman was trying to feed him. Jed shook his head and looked beyond her. He was still in Joseph Bear's tepee. Outside, the howling, demented winds of winter still prowled. Inside was the familiar smell of Indian.

He tried to say something. Sable Hair Woman held the spoon hopefully up to his mouth. He tried to lift his head and take some, but he couldn't manage it. He closed his eyes and sank back into darkness, a darkness that rapidly became disordered nightmares. In a thousand ways, it seemed, Annabelle was calling to him, pleading with him to come after her, to save her.

He awoke thrashing in the darkness, aware that a searing fever was consuming him. Sable Hair Woman was trying to cool him with chunks of ice packed inside strips of blankets, but it seemed to do little good. His teeth chattered wildly. His head seemed ready to burst. He flung off the ice packs and plunged back into another wild sleep.

When next he awoke, he was aware of Sable Hair Woman lying on his chest, her loose hair covering his face and neck with a dark veil. Through it he could barely see her sleek body gleaming with perspiration. He felt her hand guiding his fiery erection into her. She leaned suddenly back, shaking her black penumbra of hair out behind her. He saw her small, taut breasts, the nipples straining forward. Then she sank forward, dropped her head to his chest, and clung to him.

He quivered wildly, shouting, screaming, half out of his mind until he exploded deep within her. Again and again, he came. He grew drunk with it, and all the while she clung to him. His fury subsided. Perspiration began to pour in rivulets off him. Only dimly was he aware of Sable

Hair Woman hugging him tightly as a deep, dreamless sleep claimed him at last.

Jed was sitting on a knoll drinking in the April sun when Tom Fitz appeared on his mule. The old trapper waved when he saw Jed catch sight of him. Jed didn't get up as Tom Fitz rode closer. He was well enough, but still weak. It would be another week or so before he could ride.

Without dismounting, Tom Fitz pulled to a halt and gazed down at Jed. "Well, hoss, you done kilt yourself a fair number of redskins, that's for sure."

Jed peered up at Tom Fitz without comment.

"Thing is, you got to see if they ain't a better way."

"For what?"

"For getting back yore sister."

"I'll get her."

"Just came by to tell you what I heard."

"I'm listening."

"Tall Buffalo's made her his principal wife. He says Golden Hawk is dead."

"He'll find out different."

"What about them Comanches still after you?"

"Let them come."

"Why not let her be, Jed? I don't suppose Tall Buffalo is treating her poorly. Word is, she gets anything she wants. He puts a great store by her."

"She was taken by force, Tom. The Blackfeet are not her people."

"Give her time."

"Thanks for stoppin' by, Tom."

Tom Fitz gathered up his reins and pulled his mule around. Then he looked back at Jed. "That stream where you kilt the bear is good beaver country. Maybe, if you get a chance, you could join me, hoss."

"Maybe. Thanks, Tom."

As Tom Fitz rode back the way he had come, Sable Hair Woman climbed the knoll and came to a halt beside Jed. She had learned enough English during his long convalescence to converse easily with him.

"Mountain man want you to go trap beaver with him?"

"He thinks I should leave my sister with Tall Buffalo. He thinks it would be best."

"What you think?" He could feel the hope in her voice.

"She's my sister. I'll take her from the Blackfeet."

"Yes," she said sadly. "You must do that. And I will stay here with my father. Remember, the Nez Percé honor Golden Hawk."

He took her hand. "I won't leave for a while yet."

Sable Hair Woman sat down beside him, resting her head against his shoulder, saying nothing more. After a while she got up and walked back down the knoll to her father's lodge. Jed watched Joseph Bear greet her; then he looked northward, into Blackfoot country.

The Blackfoot thought he was dead. He'd let

Tall Buffalo think that for a while longer and then he'd visit their land again.

He couldn't do otherwise. In every breath of wind, every cry of the eagle circling overhead, even in the rush of the spring freshets—Jed heard only one voice, that of his sister, Annabelle, calling to him. Until he found her again and brought her back to her people, he couldn't rest.

He lifted his head to see the thin green of the new foliage covering the slopes. Spring was close and Sable Hair Woman had assured him summer would follow in this high country with a suddenness that would surprise him. From his pocket he took a whetstone and from his sheath his throwing knife.

Then he began to sharpen it.

Wild Westerns by Warren T. Longtree

**Buy them at your local
bookstore or use coupon
on next page for ordering.**